Acknowledgments-

Without help and encouragement from the following people I would never have written, or if I had written I would never have published, these tales. In no particular order muchas gracias to: John Clevenger, Pam Pryzbylo, Billy Finn, Paul Maritz, David Lundquist, Zola Stoltz, Luigi Chiarani, Tim Roska, Dori Vialpando, Tadeo Poderes, Chris and Kathleen Talbot, Bill and Terry Cummings, Kenny Brown, John Kemmeries, and the Circuit Writers of Portal, Arizona. Gracias amigos! Special thanks to Gordon Stitt for many great photos.

83rd edition copyright © by 2010 John Quinn Olson

ISBN 0-9820703-4-9 Paperback
ISBN 0-9820703-5-2 Hardcover

Published for you by

Dust Devil Press

Rodeo, NM

Cover art by David Lundquist
www.EagleEyeStudio.com

Tales From The Wild Blue Yonder
Taking Mexico Flying
By John Quinn Olson

This book is dedicated to all those people who speak and write Español better than I. Please, forgive me!

Playa, voladores and chavos, somewhere in Mexico.

A man can do worse than to relive the part of his life that's pure Technicolor.
--Clifford Irving

~~~~~~

Cover photo: Over San Blas with Miguel
Bahia Matanchen in the background

~~~~~~~~~~~~~~~~~~~~~~~ _____ ~~~~~~~~~~~~~~~~~~~

-Table Of Contents-

Antagonize not the dragons, for thou art crunchy to them, and taste of chicken.
--Confucius

~~~~~~~~~~~~~~~~~~~~~~~~——————~~~~~~~~~~~~~~~~

Forward, Taking MEXICO Flying

Sure the gringo was going to fly. He was looking at five months in Mexico—maybe six—where he would likely get a hundred days or more of great soaring. Who knew the future—maybe he would never return. So, he was going to need some reading material. Plenty to read in fact, and he would have to bring the books himself. Heck, nobody reads anything down there, or so it seemed to the gringo.

That was an exaggeration of course, but there was no doubt books were more easily found in Gringolandia, that bookstores were rare in Mexico and libraries, well… Walter had never visited a public library in all of Mexico. Maybe there were lending libraries in Mexico, but not like in the States. In fact, about all the flier had ever seen for reading material in Mexico were the daily newspapers and those silly comic books the peasants read.

He swung his pickup off the street and into the parking lot at Title Wave Books in Tucson, Arizona. This was his last chance to load up on books, and since they were all used books he could really go wild and spend very little. He was hoping to add to his collection of books on Mexico that he was forever hauling around. He loved the idea of going flying in Mexico with Mexico books.

Parking his truck now, he climbed in back under the rack full of wings, and threw open the secret compartment where he stored his tools, spare parts and his own personal library, and took a quick inventory. If he found some duplicates in Title

Wave, and they were cheap enough, he would buy them and give them away. He had a fair collection:

The Conquest Of New Spain, by Bernal Diaz de Castillo; billed as the first book actually penned in the New World, the gringo saw it as essential reading for any Mexico nut.

Aztec, by Gary Jennings, a fellow gringo with a fabulous imagination, his book is the story of the same conquest, but as seen through the eyes of a loveable Aztec—a really great read.

Feathered Serpent, by Colin Falconer, another conquest-of-Mexico tale that Walter just could not put down.

The King's Cavalier, by Samuel Shellabarger—yet another great story of the conquest.

Distant Neighbors: a Portrait of the Mexicans, by Alan Riding. This very readable history is based on the premise that there are no two nations anywhere on Earth, that share a common border, and yet are so socio/economically and culturally divergent as Mexico and the United States.

Fire And Blood: A History of Mexico, a very heavy history by T.R. Fehrenbach—who brings the reader along from the pre-Aztecs whom the author calls 'Amer-Indians,' up to the assassination of Luis Colosio in 1994.

The People's Guide To Mexico, by Lorena Havens and Carl Franz, a great and zany guidebook with adventures.

Tom Mix And Pancho Villa, A Romance, by Clifford Irving, a fabulous yarn that brings the Mexican revolution of 1910 to life.

The Tortilla Curtain, by T. C. Boyle, which is not actually about Mexico at all but sort of.

~~~~~~~~~~~~~~~~~~~~ _____ ~~~~~~~~~~~~~~

Like Water For Chocolate, by Laura Esquivel—a love story with recipes.

He had a fairly good Mexico stash, but pretty much anything that looked like entertainment he would score from Title Wave and throw in; he just needed good reading. Reading and flying, after all, were two enduring passions in his life.

"Do you have a Mexico section?" he asked the clerk.

"Of course," he replied. "Down here by the the border we sell a ton of books on Mexico. Heck, we've even got a Spanish language section."

He led the gringo around the corner and down some isles and pointed.

"Gracias," said the flier and immediately a title waved at him:

Mexico, by James Michener.

Walter had read plenty of Michener and was somewhat bored with him but he had to hand it to the author—he was wildly successful. Plus, his books were usually big, as was this one—over two thousand pages. He pulled it off the shelf and right away decided, *I'll take it.* He wasn't sure how he'd missed it so far, but it would keep him busy and it certainly was appropriate for the impending journey. Maybe **Mexico** was just that book he could throw in his harness and take flying so he'd always have something to read no matter where he landed.

He spent an hour perusing the stacks of used books at Title Wave and left with a heavy sack of them for six bucks. He got back to the truck and opened his library again and tossed the books in. He kept **Mexico** aside and threw it in his harness bag, zipped it inside for when the time came. It looked like now he would be taking **Mexico** flying, quite literally.

He glanced again at his growing library of Mexico. He craved something more but didn't know what, until a brief thought crossed his brain like: *Wouldn't it be great to contribute something of my own to Mexico reading someday?*

Well, it seemed rather unlikely but ¿quien sabe? He certainly had a subject in mind—hang gliding. Only mankind's most ancient dream, that's all; to fly with the birds.

To spread feathery wings and climb effortlessly across the sky and gaze regally down upon the masses.

To reach out a hand and touch the face of God.

To turn arduous journeys into larks.

And heck, he was the gringo who knew Mexico best from the sky. He was the gringo who was getting to know Mexico like no other gringo ever had the pleasure—from above.

Heck too, not even Feathered Serpent—Quetzalcóatl himself—had ever come to know Mexico from above quite like this gringo.

He fired up the Ford and peeled out of the bookstore parking lot. He merged in traffic for I-19 south, hot for the border. He stepped on the gas and quickly hit cruise speed. He was a happy gringo

and he went rocking down the highway.

By God! He was taking **Mexico** flying.

Poor Mexico, so far from God,
so close to the United States.
--Porfirio Díaz

Big John Comes To Valle de Bravo or, A Gringo Lands In Heaven

Big John felt like a carrot in a pepper crate as the crowded bus pulled into Valle de Bravo. Towering over the other occupants, and pale from a long Ohio winter, he could feel the natives staring at him as though he was a freak of nature. One child, a babe in arms, alternated between sucking on his mother's large brown nipple and waving a pinkie at Big John's big blonde head.

It had been an arduous journey thus far, one that had been postponed a day due to heavy surface fog back in Cincinnati, fog that had grounded all flight departures. Consequently, Big John had arrived in Mexico City a day late, had missed his group of gringos, and had to make the trip from the airport to the bus terminal and on to Valle as a solo gringo. He used the fact sheet Walter had supplied to make the trip easier and was now pulling into town to end the journey.

According to the brochure from Safari Sky Tours, "The adventure begins when you land...!" So far this had been an understatement. But if he could just locate this place called... er, uhhm... Papa... lót... zin, a sporting-goods shop and the local hang gliding center, everything would turn out okay he was sure. The gringo just hoped Papalótzin was easier to locate than it was to say.

Big John, in his excitement, was among the first to step off the bus. The locals, most of whom were much smaller than Big John, wisely yielded to his rush for the door. The first thing he noticed was that the afternoon temperature was hot, yet very agreeable. Casting his glance towards the sky he saw beautiful cumulous cloud streets heading out of town and his spirits soared. He searched through his pockets, found the last page of instructions for arriving at Papalótzin, and examined them carefully. There was a map on one side explaining directions. On the other side was a single word, in large bold print:

-ZOCALO-

Big John held the page up to the bus driver and said, "Señor...."

The bus driver beheld the gringo and his cryptic message and pointed down the street.

Liberated now, and ready to stretch his legs, shouldering his harness and lugging his luggage, Big John commenced the final walk to his destination. He rounded the first corner and was startled by an armed soldier in full combat gear, toting an automatic weapon in front of the Banco de Mexico. Warily unfamiliar with such a spectacle, and somewhat troubled by it, he crossed the street to continue on, with a suspicious sidelong glance to see if he would draw fire. He approached a taco stand that was doing a brisk business on the street, and was overwhelmed by a savory roasted aroma of beef and onions and pineapple that set his stomach to growling. But at about the same moment he banged his head sharply on the awning as he walked past—kerthunk, twang!

The patrons seemed not surprised at all by such a spectacle, but Big John cursed his luck and staggered on. Raising a hand to his forehead, it came away with a spot of blood. He cursed again but kept moving; Big John Leek had just suffered his first-ever "Mexicanazo".

He threaded his way through a village market set up on the street, where all sorts of strange things were on sale. As he dabbed his bleeding forehead with a clean hankie that his wife had insisted he bring along, he was forced to stoop this way and that to avoid more bloodshed—everything seemed to be erected with a midget in mind.

At the end of the market he encountered several butcher shops where long strips of animal meat hung in the sun and buzzed with flies. The sight of large carcasses hanging in such gruesome style spurred Big John's sense of adventure a notch... He picked up the pace an equal measure.

He was glad then as, following his map, he rounded a corner and came into what must be the Zocalo, a tree shaded plaza with an ancient church dominating one side, with shops and restaurants set along the perimeter. He looked to the north and there among the other shops he spotted it: *Papalótzin* read the sign. A colorful windsock hung limp in the still, tropical air.

Big John walked up the stairs and into the shop. The hang glider suspended from the rafters greeted him when he walked through the door and he knew he had arrived at the right place. A friendly Mexican walked up and shook hands with Big John. He gazed with interest at Big John's bleeding forehead and handed him a fresh Kleenex.

"Is Walter here?" inquired the gringo.

Without answer, but beckoning with a finger, the clerk handed Big John the microphone from a two-way radio base station concealed behind the counter. Big John took the mic and looked at the clerk. The clerk gestured again and smiled at the gringo. "Andale!" he said. *Go ahead!*

Big John keyed the mic and spoke tentatively into it. "Ahhh..." he began. "Is...is anyone there?"

~🄽≥≤🄽~

Ten miles away, at eight thousand feet, Walter hung comfortably in his harness and scratched-out from a cornfield in a marginal thermal. His other pilots were strung out behind him, some already grounded, some eager to catch up. He worked the thermal with a buzzard that was not faring much better. Given another thousand feet and Walter had a clear shot for the landing field on the lake in Valle. He might make even it now if he went for it, depending on the air he encountered between here and there. As he was eyeballing the glide angle his two-way radio suddenly sparked to life with a new, yet familiar, voice.

"Ahhh..." it said, "Is...is anyone there?"

Walter grabbed the microphone—this was good news. All Walter's pilots for Safari Sky Tours had arrived safely yesterday, with the exception of Big John Leek—a pasty-white gringo extraordinaire— who had gone missing somewhere between Cleveland or Cincinnati and Mexico City. Walter recognized his voice even through the ether. Big John, if he'd followed directions, would have $700 tucked safely in his boot for Walter, to pay for a week of south-of-the-border flying adventure.

It was PAYDAY!

"Big John!" he called into the radio. "Got a copy?"

"Walter...is that you?" The voice was up-tempo, relieved.

"Yes indeedy amigo mio. I guess you musta found the shop."

"Oh man... am I glad to be here. That was some bus ride! Whooee!"

"Did everything go all right?"

"Well, I'm bleeding slightly. No biggie."

Bleeding? Walter pointed his Airwave glider along the radio waves towards town and stretched his glide to take advantage of a slight tailwind. Meanwhile, he gave John some simple instructions: "Antonio—the amigo working the shop—he's got the key to my house, Juan. Follow the Airwave bumper stickers as you see 'em going down the street and on down the hill. There's an Airwave sticker on the front door, too. Just follow the stickers and I'll call you when you get there!"

"Where are you?" asked Juan Grande.

"I've just broke ten grand and I'm on glide for the landing area," replied Walter. "I'll be landing near the casa."

"Right on Walter!" said the gringo. "I'll wait for you at your casa!"

Juan Grande left Papalótzin and right away noticed an Airwave Gliders bumper sticker high on a power pole. He trudged along under the hot sun and, arriving at the first sticker, located another on the side of a house a stone's throw distant. From there he found another and yet another until, walking down an impossibly steep and narrow cobblestone street, he came to Walter's casa. With another identifying Airwave bumper sticker on the door, there could be little doubt.

~~~~~~~~~~~~~~~ ～～～～～～～～～～～～～

Kind of like Snow White or Hansel and Gretel or whomever it was who threw those bread crumbs to mark the way home, he thought. *Maybe the three dwarves.*

He unlocked the door to enter and immediately knew he was in the right place by the stack of gliders waiting inside. Just then, another radio startled him.

"Big John," it squawked. "Calling Juan Grande. Do you read me Juan?"

John saw a radio sitting on the dining room table. He grabbed it and spoke in the affirmative. "I read you Walter. Cool place. Nice view of the lake!"

The Lake.

Walter was not going to make the lake as things were going. He had not enough altitude to cross over the ridge at La Torre and glide to the lake. Instead he was forced to circle again in some marginal lift. But he was slowly climbing out over Mesón Viejo. He could barely see over the ridge top to the landing area now. Maybe he could fly around the ridge rather than fly over it? But a few more circulos gained him a few more hundreds of feet, until final glide was a piece of pastel. Walter keyed the mic and called to Big John on the ground and the other tiny dots in the sky.

"I think I've got the lake made," he said. "I'm going into town. See you guys there!" He pulled on the bar and leveled the wing, gliding over the ridge towards payday.

"Hey Juan," he called, "You see the refrigerator in there?"

"¡Sí señor!" came the response.

"Look see if there are cervesas inside."

"¡Sí señor!" Juan replied with gusto. He was really getting into this Spanish lingo... He flung the 'fridge open and found it stuffed with ice-cold beer.

"How many you think you can carry?" asked the radio.

"All of 'em," laughed Juan Grande. "But I might need some help."

"Just fill your pockets and grab what you can," radioed Walter. "Do you notice that soccer field out the front window? Grab the radio and the cervesa and meet me there."

A loud whoop! came out Walter's radio as Big John followed his instructions. He pulled the casa door shut and sprinted down the hill to the soccer field. From Walter's vantage he could see the big gringo stride briskly out onto the field, laden with refreshing beverages and already quenching his thirst on a chilled Corona.

"That's me gliding in from the mountains," he called. He flew over the field with enough altitude left for an approach. He turned into the wind and aimed for a stop just before the big gringo with the beer. With a mighty flare, he settled to earth just THERE!

"Welcome to Hang Glide Heaven, amigo!" he said.

Juan Grande let out another WHOOP!, a whoop of joy and happiness. He handed his old amigo a beer. "Man Walter!" he exclaimed. "It's good to be here!"

Flight To The Heavenly Water or,
A Twenty Peso Bargain

A dozen colorful wings were once again spread atop a cliff on the steep side of Cerro Grande, a towering mountain outside of Colima City in the central Mexican heartland. A Mexican polka danced raucously from the dashboard of a nearby pickup truck while the wings were stretched, the ribs were stuffed and the wires were tensioned. Occasionally, a brave soul would sidle up to the precipice just a few short steps away, and stick a hand into the vertical blast of air, checking it out.

To an observer who might happen along to witness this daily ritual, the thermals might sound a bit like an eighteen-wheeler as they roar up past the launch ramp. A family of buzzards dove in below launch to hook the thermal and one by one, went spiraling silently into the blue sky above the flyers and disappeared. The buzzards did not go unnoticed as they soared aloft, but not much was said over the music; the flyers were intent on making all preparations for another day of flying. The sweltering tropical sun made every movement a bit of a struggle for at least one gringo, but it was shaping up as yet another bitchin' day over Cerro Grande.

A raucous rook came diving into the thermal and circled out noisily above the flyers gathered below— making as much racket as one single bird might. "FOOLS!" he seemed to cry; "Fools Fools Fools!"

Clipped into his wing now, all suited up for altitude and sweating like an army mule, Walter approached the edge of the cliff on Cerro Grande very cautiously, with an amigo holding each wing wire, until he was standing in front of a narrow steel launch ramp. The incline jutted out from the cliff at a steep angle and ended in the sky. It was about three giant steps long. A ripping thermal wagged his wings dangerously, so Pedro and Benigno grabbed at his wires and brought his wings back to level. Walter was grunting with effort to control and balance the wings when suddenly, they were light as a feather and tugging at him in eagerness.

"Clear!" he hollered.

"CLEAR!" came the chorus from his launch crew as they released his wires.

With another grunt Walter took three giant-steps with his nose pointed sharply down the cliff. But only one toe scratched the ramp below as the thermal blasted him into the sky. In a flash he was off the mountain cleanly, wings level, airspeed roaring... WahOOO! Another day of flight was underway in the skies above Mexico.

Counting to ten, the gringo banked the wing up and dug in to a fierce column of rising air right in front of launch. With a shot of adrenaline coursing through his brain he headed for the Heavens Above. Down below, the scramble was ON!

Walter climbed out above the launch ramp, and watched the activity below as his amigos del cielo all scrambled for their harnesses, clipped into their wings, and eagerly bailed for the sky. Before long they were but tiny little dots below him, each one circling in their own private dance of the thermals, and everyone climbing for the clouds. It was just too good!

This particular day Walter climbed quite high above Cerro Grande. Having launched at about twenty-five hundred feet, he soon topped-out at near ten grand. The sky was particularly clear today and the smoking fire volcano Colimótl was offering a spectacular show in the near distance, crouched and puffing like a smoldering god on the horizon.

Having gained such lofty heights Walter decided to cash in on them; perhaps today was the day to try to make the glide all the way back home to the airfield at the Flying Club of Colima. So he aimed his nose at the distant far edge of Colima town, leveled the wings with the bar at his chest, and commenced a long unlikely glide figuring *what the heck—nothing ventured, nothing gained.*

It soon became quite clear however that Walter would have to either find another thermal or get a better glide somewhere along the line, or he would come up short of the refreshing swimming pool at his destination. The magic spot that only the flyer can see while he is on glide—the spot he's gliding to—was a bit shy of the airfield. Pointing his toes, tucking in his elbows, Walter went for the glide anyway. But it was not to be...

Gliding over fields and villages, getting lower and lower, coming up short of the airstrip, Walter finally chickened-out. If he held his present course he would come up about two fields shy of success. He might be able to glide blindly into a strange field and land successfully or... or he might not. He might arrive over the unfamiliar field and discover some obstacle that would complicate his landing or otherwise ruin his day; a fence or power lines or a ditch. Perhaps the field would be plowed or full of cattle. That mental picture was too grim to dwell on. One thing was certain though: the flyer would get only one chance at success. He cranked a shallow turn to larboard and began a close inspection of the field he was directly over, flying a pattern for a safe landing.

As a concession to convenience, Walter made one glance about him looking for the easy way out of this field once he'd packed-up. All he could see for certain was a housing development off to the east. Then, with a quick turn from base-to-final, he stuffed the bar and came blazing in. Diving in to the field now and roaring over a few startled burros, Walter gave the bar a big heave and flared to a stop. Gently, he settled to the ground as though stepping off his bar stool. The flight had not been a total success, but it had been action-packed and disaster-free.

Now to pack up his wing and gear in their bags and get home somehow...

~Ɽ≥≤Ɽ~

Grunting with effort and slipping and sliding in the loose dirt, the gringo dragged his wing up the steep arroyo as best he could. He'd been forced to leave his gear bag behind him in the bottom of the gully while he dragged his Wills Wing Fusion first down the steep bank, then up the other side. There, he'd been confronted with a barbed-wire fence. Shoving the glider nose-first between the ground and the lowest strand of wire, Walter'd had to groan and curse with effort to keep the wing moving, and to keep himself from pitching backwards into the hole. With another curse to the Sky Gods and to whoever cabron had invented barbed wire, he shoved the wing under the rusty old strands and scurried under with it.

Once the wing was under the wire he'd been able to grab on and drag it completely clear of the fence and over a few mounds of dirt where he took a bit of a breather. Then, in what he hoped to be the last time for one day, he shouldered his burden once again, and trudged like some grimey and unlikely pilgrim to the edge of a street. He unloaded the wing from his shoulder and dropped to his knees in exhaustion. He had some notion how Jesus himself must have suffered his burden so long ago. He drained the last few drops of agua from his bottle and clambered back over the fence to fetch his gear bag.

By the time Walter had returned to his wing, having scrambling through the arroyo yet again and through thorn bushes and over hill and dale, he was spent, dirty and most of all—parched. His shirt was torn from the rusty barbed wire and he was bleeding too, from a nasty thorn that had pierced his shin and broken off. He'd had to grab the thorn with his fingernails and yank it out. In fact, it seemed to the gringo that everything in the Mexican bush came with a thorn or a barb attached. Either that, or it bit, stung or itched.

Examining his surroundings he discovered that his ordeal had brought him smack into the middle of a construction zone. He really wasn't on a street at all, more of a dusty work-access area. Tough-looking Mexican hard-hat types were eyeballing him from various locations; suspicion and scorn written across some faces, curiosity and glee on others.

"¿Que pasa con este pinche gringo?" they seemed to say, and "What the chingada do you suppose he has in those bags?"

But Walter didn't care—he was just too spent. He'd survived certain disaster after all, defied the Grim Reaper once again and lived through it, flung himself from the heights and slipped the surly bonds of Earth. What could be more uncertain back on the planet? Besides, things always seem to sort themselves out here in old Mexico.

He was alive! It was all that mattered.

For twenty years now people, mostly other gringos who had no idea what the hell they were talking about, had been warning Walter to stay the hell away from Mexico. Bad things, terrible things it seemed, happened to gringos who wandered around down there. But Walter was too dumb or too stubborn to worry about these rumors. It was the flying that called on him to travel south. The rest of it would work itself out and sure enough, just then the miracle happened.

Oh, it was a tiny miracle, the type of miracle that happens many thousands of times a day just in Colima alone. Must be millions of times each day in the whole country he supposed; maybe then, not a miracle at all—just a chance encounter. But as Walter plunked himself down on a pile of rubble in the shade of a stately primavera tree... the Cielo truck turned the corner and headed straight for the suffering gringo. Not much of a bible-thumper, Walter was grateful nonetheless.

"¡Gracias al cielo!" he declared to himself, to no one, to everyone. *Thank the Heavens!*

Now, the word 'cielo' means 'sky' in Español, but it also means 'heaven'. In fact in Mexican Español 'sky' seems a rather forgotten word, lost in a pious Catholic frenzy, and 'heaven' prevails. In fact, for most Catholic Mexicans 'cielo' is far more than just that big blue thing overhead—'cielo' is Heaven. 'Cielo' is where God himself allegedly resides as He watches down upon us all. 'Cielo' is where everyone—you, and I, and everyone else—hopes to some day end up. It is much the same as in English where we sometimes refer to our sky as 'the Heavens' only less so.

But in Mexico, 'Cielo' is also a brand of bottled water, a beverage owned by the Coca Cola bottling company and sold all over the country, from trucks you are likely to encounter just about anywhere. It was one of these rumbling beasts that turned the corner now, and made a dusty beeline for the thirsty gringo, in what he saw as a bit of a miracle. Agua del Cielo—Heavenly Water—is sold in many different size bottles, but the truck Walter now beheld carried only the giant twenty-liter jugs called *garafones*, and meant especially for residential use.

Like a rusty blessing from above the Cielo truck rumbled up to the gringo, who stood slowly to his feet and beckoned the driver to a halt.

"¡Por favor!" he begged. *Please!*

The driver threw the tranny into park and shut down the spark. Suddenly all was blessedly quiet and tranquil in Walter's life. Birds chirped in the primavera tree, the dust settled, and the promise of refreshment was but a moment away.

"Favor que tomo uno," he told his savior while fumbling with a grubby wad of pesos and gazing up at the truck. *Please, I'll take one.*

The driver, a bearded man with thick shoulder-length silver hair, a man who looked like no one so much as Moses in one of those heavenly frescos you see from Michaelangelo, popped the door handle and crawled down from on high. He stepped down from the running board and walked about the Earth like a mortal man. He tugged a heavenly garafon off the rack and shouldered it carefully, like the Holy burden it was. He looked here, and he looked there, wondering where amongst the footings and holes and walls and piles of dirt, to put it.

Where do you suppose the gringo wanted his agua?

"¿Como sale el puro liquido?" asked the gringo. *How much for just the water only?*

Walter may have been feeling blessed, but economics were still an issue and he had no interest in acquiring the bottle, a container which actually cost somewhat more than the contents. Besides, he didn't need the bottle—he needed a drink. The Cielo driver was confused but gave the standard reply.

"Vente pesos," he said *Twenty pesos.*

"Da me lo," repeated the gringo. *Give it to me.* But the driver was still confused.

"¿Donde?" he asked, peering about. *Where?* There was no kitchen counter, there was no pantry shelf. There was no clever water dispenser to cradle the garafon as found in all Mexican casas. There was no casa either, for that matter. There was only dust and dirt and rubble. Where would he put it?

"¿Donde?" he asked again. *Where?*

"Aqui," replied the gringo... *Here.* He doffed his sweaty sombrero and pointed to his sweaty head.

The driver smiled at that notion. He laughed when Walter simply sat down on the nearest rock and kept pointing at his head. "¡Da me lo!" he commanded, but he had to say it twice more... "¡Da me lo señor! ¡Favor da me lo!"

The driver tore open the lid, grinning now. Tentatively, he poured a little glug down Walter's open mouth and throat. The water splashed down the gringo's chest with a delightful chilling effect. Walter gasped and commanded once again, "¡Da me lo," he said. "Da me cada gota!" *Give me every drop!*

Suddenly, the driver didn't look like Moses any more. He was laughing now and smiling, and he tipped the Heavenly garafon over Walter's head with mucho gusto.

"Gulg glug glug," went the bottle.

"Splash splash splash," went the Heavenly water.

"Gulp gulp gulp," went the lucky gringo.

The Cielo driver was quite happy now; perhaps he had never dispensed his product quite like this— a sort of impromptu baptismo for a pagan gringo alongside the Camino of Life. Walter was happy too—fulfilled so to speak. Even the tough-hombre worker types on the construction jobs seemed to be refreshed.

Soon the water emptied from the garafon and the driver shook the last few drops on Walter's soggy head. It left the gringo refreshed, water sloshing around in his belly, a puddle of mud all about him.

It seemed as though, with a bit of Heavenly intervention, he'd live to fly yet another day.

Let me ride on the ride of death one more time
Let me ride on the ride of death one more time
You can waste your time on the other rides
But this is the nearest to being alive
Oh! Let me take my chances on the ride of death
~~~~~~~~~~~~~

Mauricio Skys Out or,
Miracle At Rock Of The Devil

"Favor que presta me un ala," said my amigo Mauricio. *Please lend me a wing.*

They were words that brought me very mixed emotions. On the one hand I had great respect for Mauricio—he had taught me to fly trikes after all. And he was a glidehead from Way-Back, supposedly among the first in Valle de Bravo. It could not have been easy to learn to fly in the central highlands of Mexico—a high place and a mountainous place and a place far from any flight training centers. Furthermore, the launch over the

~~~~~~~~~~~~~~~~~~ ~~~~~~~~~~~~~~~~~

lake from a ridge called La Torre required a landing approach over deep water and a touch-down in a small grassy field. It must have been intimidating for any beginner, yet Mauricio had indeed learned to fly there. Thus my respect for his judgment and skills.

My anxiety stemmed from the fact that Mauricio had not flown a hang glider in five years and never at all from the ripping thermal site outside of town called El Peñon del Diablo—The Rock of the Devil. The launch had not even been cut from the forest when Mauricio was a Valle flyer. Flying from El Peñon was not the smooth lake-effect experience of a flight from La Torre above town. El Peñon would require greater pilot skills to fly successfully, and if the flyer went down and was forced to land in the baking valley two thousand feet below, he would be dealing with small rocky fields and ferocious thermals—dust devils maybe. It was always best to get high at El Peñon, and stay high all the way home to Valle de Bravo.

Did Mauricio have it in him? I couldn't say for sure. Nor could his wife, the look of concern she gave me only accented my own.

For his part, Mauricio had little doubt. If he could just get his hands on a wing he knew what he had to do.

"Favor que presta me un ala," he said again. *Please lend me a wing.*

Mauricio had plenty of self-confidence, what he lacked was a hang glider of his own. At the moment of his request I was loading the Ford-From-Hell with a stack of hang gliders; beautiful state-of-the-art sailcloth from Pacific Airwave in Salinas, California. PacAir had entrusted me with this stack of wings, sent me south for my annual pilgrimage to central Mexico as a flying guide, in hopes that I would someday return with them and meanwhile generate more sales than I would wreckage. I could imagine my benefactor Kenny Brown's face even now as I loaded another of his wings atop the Ford and meanwhile assured my amigo Mauricio that I would load one for him too.

"You'll be happy with a Vision Mark IV," I said, naming a very mellow wing. I had a group of New Yorkers who were in Mexico to fly my gliders for a week, and they had first choice of wings. I knew they'd want the hot ships.

"Lo que sobre," smiled Mauricio happily. *Whatever is left.* His lovely wife Patricia tried to smile just as happily, but I could see the spirit was not really there. She would have preferred her husband just stand around the mountaintop with the rest of the spectators—and with his wife and child—instead of joining in the dangerous fun. But she knew there was no changing the plan. Her hombre was hot to fly.

As I mentioned, Mauricio had no wing of his own, which is why he wanted to borrow one of mine. But he also had no harness to suspend himself in the wing, no helmet or parachute to protect himself from the wing and no flight instruments to assist in making his flight a success. He was going to have to borrow all this stuff, and he was going to have to borrow it all from me.

I felt a bit foolish then, as I stuffed all the necessary gear in a bag and handed it to my amigo. I knew that what we were contemplating was contrary to one of the most basic rules of common sense associated with any high-risk adventure, the rule that states:

Only One New Risk Element At A Time.

I would be sending Mauricio out in a wing he had never flown, in a harness he had never flown, at a launch he had never flown. We'd have three strikes against us the moment my amigo's feet left Terra Firma.

I looked to Patricia as we loaded into the Ford-From-Hell and I could see she was putting up a happy façade. She held their daughter Johanna in her arms and we all set sail out of Valle, my amigos up front in the cab with me, my gringos and a few other local voladores crammed in back and maintaining a constant excited chatter. At least part of my trepidation resulted from Patricia and Johanna—Mauricio's family. It would have all been much easier to throw him into such uncertainty if Mauricio did not have such a lovely familia. But his wife was about the most stunningly beautiful woman I had ever seen, and their two-year-old daughter was too cute for words.

Patricia was tall and willowy, she had gorgeous brown feet with perfect red toenails, lovely legs like flower stems, a curvaceous figure to make any man wonder, a slender neck that held aloft a beautiful head and a face to die for, lips like twin strawberries. She carried herself in a graceful manner and when she smiled the whole world seemed to smile with her. She had a flawless complexion—skin like cinnamon—and she always smelled fresh and well... female. She was weaning her child too, which lent her a certain bountiful appeal as well. It was difficult not to gaze at my amigo's lovely wife and child. I found myself in conflict with one of those ten commandments that Moses had reportedly brought down from the Mount—the one that declares THOU SHALT NOT COVET THY AMIGO'S WIFE.

I'm afraid I'd had a crush on Patricia from that moment years ago when first my eyes met hers.

Now here she was, brushing lightly up against me, holding her child in her lap as the Ford jostled us while we rocked and rolled out of Valle de Bravo and up the mountain road on the way to the Rock of the Devil. I knew she was even more anxious than I about the events that would soon come to pass.

"Ahh!" enthused Mauricio with a glance out the window. "Muy buen dia pa volar!" He tapped a ritmo on the dashboard along with Carlos Santana. *It's a great day to fly!*

~ɲ≥≤ɲ~

"CLEAR!" hollered Voighter as he steadied the wing against the thermal that was rolling up the natural slope launch called El Peñon del Diablo. We don't actually launch from the devilish rock itself; the launch slope is atop the rim of an ancient volcanic caldera, part of which is an extinct lava dome that dominates the view out front—the Rock of the Devil himself. Voighter steadied the wing for a moment, glanced right and left to make sure he was free of all fetters, and then charged down the slope for three hard steps, meeting that thermal head-on. A few tiny puffs of dirt punctuated his run and then the wing lifted him gracefully into the sky. He immediately began a climb that would not end for a half hour or so, at which point he would be high above launch, and the Rock of the Devil would be a harmless obelisk far below.

"Next!" I hollered although it was hardly necessary. JayJay, Bobo, Carlos, Roger and Jolly Bill were all cued up eagerly behind me. They were clipped in to their wings and making a few last-minute adjustments to helmets, gloves, flight decks and sunglasses. We could all hear the Voighter's flight deck screaming with glee from somewhere overhead—and becoming fainter as he climbed-out.

JayJay lifted his wing and carried it the last few steps up to launch. His gaze went right through me as he studied the conditions out front while I helped to steady his wing. We performed one final hang check to make sure he was properly connected to the wing, and then JayJay picked up his weapon. He steadied it against the thermal just as Voighter had done, and then he looked me in the eye.

"Clear!" he hollered.

I let go his wing then, and dove out of his way. He hesitated only a moment and then took those same steps as his compadre had only moments before.

Suddenly, there were two gringos climbing out in the sky above Mexico.

"¡Proximo!" I hollered. *Next!*

And so it went as Bobo, Carlos, Roger and Jolly Bill flung themselves into the Heavens and commenced to climb. They were joined by Brian and Santiago and Werner—locals who knew the site better than anyone. At El Peñon del Diablo, the soaring was definitely ON!

"Last!" called Mauricio, who was still back in the glider set-up area with his lovely family, and needed a little assist from his guide—myself. I was eager to join in the fun, but I was worried about Mauricio, so I had instructed him that I would help all my gringos into the sky, and then give my undivided attention to him. I turned to that chore now and I clipped him into my big yellow Vision Mark IV, performed his hang check, turned on his flight deck, and adjusted his helmet. Meanwhile Patricia watched with concern.

"Es demaciado grande," my amigo said about the brain bucket. It was true—the helmet kept falling down his forehead.

"I don't have any other suggestions," I noted.

"Lo dejo aqui entonces," he said as he started to unbuckle it. *I'll just leave it here then.*

"No!" cried Patricia and myself together.

"I'm not sending you off here without a helmet and that's that," I stated—to Patricia's obvious relief. We could hear a symphony of flight decks trilling a thrilling song overhead from our fellow flyers, who were climbing into the sky above launch. A vague shadow passed in the dirt before us as one of those gliders flew past the sun, like some high-tech Icaro beckoning us into action.

"Tampoco quiero los guantes," continued Mauricio. *I don't want the gloves either.*

That gave me an idea; "Quitate el casco por un segundo," I ordered. *Take off the helmet for a second.*

Mauricio did as I requested and handed me the bucket. It was an old thing I kept around for tandem passengers and it was supposed to be a one-size-fits-all affair, but I knew that sometimes it needed a bit of an adjustment. I peeled back the lining inside the crown and I carefully stuffed the thin gloves inside. Replacing the liner and feeling very clever about it, I handed the bucket back to my amigo.

"Prueba lo," I suggested. *Try that.*

Mauricio pulled the helmet over his head and cinched the strap very snug. He shook his head this way and that and it still seemed quite loose to me. But another shadow—or maybe the same one but a bit vaguer this time—higher—passed before us again and Mauricio nodded to me.

"¡Vamanos!" he said. *Let's go!*

Patricia followed us up to launch holding Johanna in her arms. The tiny child pointed a finger at her papa and said "¿Papa volar, Papa volar?" We all were hoping that Papa would indeed volar I'm sure, because it looked at this point like Papa was either going to volar or caer and I didn't want to think of the consequences of the latter.

"So you remember the flight plan?" I asked Mauricio.

"Take off and clear the arboles," he recited. "Turn left and count to diez." I nodded encouragement as he continued... "When the flight deck begins to sing I turn away from the hill." I nodded again. Following these instructions would get him into the bitchin' house thermal that resides at launch. After that, his destiny was in his own manos.

"¿Y entonces?" I asked. *And then?*

"¡Empujo!" he said with conviction. *I push out!*

"¡Bueno!"

These were about all the instructions I might give a first-timer at El Peñon. If we had a radio to put on the wing with Mauricio, we might have given him even more help in-flight, but he was going to be on his own out there. All we could do is pray to the Sky Gods and his sense of self-preservation for his safe delivery into the Heavens.

Together, we picked up the wing and he steadied it. A thermal ripped through launch and grabbed a wing and we struggled for control for a moment, were forced to set it down and straighten it out and try again. Mauricio grunted with effort a time or two and had to shove the helmet off his sweaty brow.

"No hay prisa," I said. *We have no hurry.*

We picked up that big yellow wing again and this time Mauricio held it perfectly balanced in his grip. The wing floated eagerly above his shoulders and he looked past me, concentrating on the air out front and his immediate future.

"Estoy listo amigo," he said. *I'm ready friend.*

He hesitated for just another moment and as the wing started nudging forward, eager to fly. Then he gave me the command we'd been awaiting with such misgivings.

"¡Libre!" he hollered.

I dove out of my amigo's way and hit the dirt below to be absolutely sure I was not an obstacle to his departure. I saw only Mauricio's feet making those little puffs in the dirt. Then I turned to watch, and I saw him lift perfectly into the blue Mexican sky—wings level, airspeed good. His daughter squealed with a joy that his wife and I did not entirely share.

"¡Papa volar!" she yelled. "¡Papa volar!"

Papa was indeed volaring now.

I turned back to the forest to get my own show on the road and I looked through Patricia. I might have grabbed her then and there, held her tight and gotten away with it under the circumstances, but I really could not face her. I had thrown her man out there and circumstances were now beyond my control. All I could do now was get suited-up quickly, and follow him. Maybe I could show him the house thermal.

I grabbed my gear and pulled it on. I clipped in and did my own standing hang-check. I pulled on my own helmet, turned on my own flight deck, picked up my own wing and headed for launch on my own.

"¡Cuidate mucho!" offered Patricia. *Be careful!*

I grunted with effort at holding the wing level—it might have been mistaken for a reply—but I just kept walking until I was quite literally out of the woods and in fresh airflow and then I started jogging. The wing felt nicely balanced so I turned up the throttle a notch and ran as hard as it would let me. In moments I was hot on Mauricio's tailfeathers and I had left Patricia, Johanna and our driver Chocho, standing in the forest on launch. I turned left and flew towards the roaring column of rising air—the house thermal—that makes El Peñon the legendary flying site it is. I watched Mauricio making wobbly turns and slowly sinking into the valley below. While everybody else was skying-out, Mauricio was sinking.

I flew into the house thermal and it hit me like a freight train. My right wing and nose popped at the same moment, shoving me at the tree-covered mountainside. I was glad to be flying an Airwave because the wing responded instantly in my hands. I pulled the nose down to gain speed, shoved my weight to starboard to turn away from trouble, and as she responded to my wishes I shoved her nose back up and commenced a sweet spiral into the sky—a climb that would take me to over thirteen thousand feet.

Helplessly, I watched as Mauricio swooped and wanged it this way and that below me. I tried to will him into the core of the thermal but the Gods would not harken to my feeble appeals. As I climbed out Mauricio got smaller and smaller, now just a tiny dot far below. I could not tell if he was sinking or hanging but one thing was certain—he was not climbing as the rest of us had. Before long I topped-out in the house thermal, now making giant circles in smooth air on top of the World.

I circled there for a while listening to my other flyers chattering over the radios. Everyone was having a great time, but I was worried over my amigo. There wasn't much else I could do though. I had supplied him with a great wing and a good harness. I had slapped a flight deck on his wing to help him climb out. I had put a helmet, for what it was worth, on his head. I had taken him to the one spot in all the central Mexico highlands where he was most likely to get very high, and I'd gotten him there for Prime Time—that magic moment when he was most likely to squirt for the clouds. I'd even given him a simple flight plan which was: get high, stay high, and fly high all the way back to Valle de Bravo, to land at the familiar lakeside field where he'd landed so many times before, so long ago.

Keeping my eye on Mauricio as best I could, I headed blindly over the back, joining my amigos for the flight to town. I watched him burbling around down there for as long as I could, but passing over the Zacamecáte I encountered another thermal that nearly ripped the bar from my claws. I turned my attention to my own survival then, commenced another spiraling climb, and I could not spot Mauricio again no matter how I searched the sky. Now my amigo really was on his own.

Miguel Gutierrez approaches Valle de Bravo. Photo setup by Freddy Yazbec

~₪≥≤₪~

I waited for JayJay to make his approach to the wonderful, if tight, landing field in Valle de Bravo and then flew an aircraft approach to follow him in. I flew downwind keeping my eye on the center of the field. I turned a baseleg that I figured I could adjust for final approach. I came around to pour on the speed and dive at the field and my calculations lined up perfectly. As JayJay carried his wing out of the way, I swooped down into ground effect and flared to a perfect stop. Once again the landing field in Valle had welcomed me like an old friend.

I was greeted by a cheer from my other amigos; those who had landed before me. Their gratitude for my having brought them to this incredible place extended to a chilly cervesa, which Bill Jolly ran out to the field and stuck in my hand before I had even popped my helmet. They all gathered around their guide and slapped each other on their collective backs, faces sunburned and lit with giant grins. The flight into Valle had been a great success, almost totally. The local flyers had also made the flight and a few were still soaring the cliffs above town—airhogs—including Voighter who had launched first.

I was of course relieved to be standing safely on the ground once again, but at the same time I was worried about my amigo Mauricio. I just hoped he had landed safely down below launch, which, apparently, was where he was headed.

I quaffed a chilly cervesa Indio and, mid-swig, I noticed my pickup traversing the hill along the highway. I was surprised but relieved to see it so soon. Chocho must have packed Mauricio and his wing up quickly in the distant landing field and raced back to town. I gave the truck a few minutes to arrive at the lake and then went to greet my friends.

So I was confused to see only Chocho and Patricia in the Ford as it arrived in the parking lot trailing a cloud of dust. Johanna was too tiny to be seen over the dash, and Mauricio must be relaxing in the back, tuckered-out from his ordeal. I let the truck swing into a parking spot and then I peered into the back. I was startled and confused when… there was no Mauricio!

"¿Que pasa?" I asked them dumbly. *What happened?*

~~~~~~~~~~~~~~~~ ~~~~~~~~~~~~~~~~

Chocho grinned his usually carefree smile at me. I noticed his new dentistry so popular in Mexico wherein the tooth is capped in silver. Chocho had sprung for the luxury treatment at the dentista and had a silver star inlaid in the tooth as well. It sparkled as he smiled at me. I looked to Patricia who wore a fake smile, a smile that only partially hid her wifely concern.

"Ya llegamos," said Chocho. *We have arrived.*

That much was obvious, but there was one amigo who had not arrived, one who was conspicuous in his absence. Suddenly Patricia and I uttered the same question at the same moment;

"¿Donde esta Mauricio?" we asked each other. *Where is Mauricio?*

Chocho just grinned some more while Patricia looked in panic out at the field. Her eyes scanned the flyers for that yellow wing, for her hombre, while I grilled Chocho.

"¿Fuiste para alla buscar él?" I asked. *Did you go there and look for him?* By 'there' of course, I meant the fields below launch.

"Porsupuesto fuimos pero no estubo él," said Chocho with a shrug. *Of course we went but he wasn't there.*

"¿Subio?" I asked. *Did he get up?*

"No se, estubo muy bajo," shrugged Chocho. *I don't know, he was very low.*

I could read the panic in Patricia's face—her man was missing in action. Her husband, the father of her child, had gone hang gliding and now... was nowhere to be found. We hurried down to the lakeshore and gazed up at La Torre where a few flyers were still soaring to and fro on the ridge.

~~~~~~~~~~~~~~~~~~~~ _____ ~~~~~~~~~~~~~~~~

There was no sign of my bright yellow Mark IV among them though. There was no sign of Mauricio.

By now the sky had developed a thick layer of clouds that were expanding from the direction of El Peñon and the blazing blue sky had become a threatening black over the back. It was the dry season in Mexico, so it was unlikely that there would be any measurable rain, but the sky back by the Rock of the Devil had an evil look about it. I was glad I wasn't up there.

Suddenly one of the New Yorkers pointed a finger up that way and said, "Who the heck is that?"

We all turned our heads and gazed aloft, following his finger, and we all chimed in as one—a happy chorus.

"Holy shit!" we said. *¡Mierda!*

For there was a tiny dot far behind the ridge, a little speck in the glowering sky, and it looked to be disappearing and then reappearing again in the wispy base of the clouds. Someone was very skyed-out up there, and headed our way... As I watched in wonder, the wing turned slightly and for just a moment one detail became wonderfully, obviously, apparent...

The dot was yellow!

The New Yorkers whooped for joy for the flyer. I didn't know whether I should shout for joy or fear. Patricia and I finally embraced with happiness, but she was faint with anxiety and I lowered her into a nearby lawn chair. The dot kept its nose pointed at us while the crowd speculated about its lofty position. Somehow my amigo had hooked into the lift at El Peñon while very low, and then taken it up to cloudbase at close to... well, we couldn't be sure... maybe fifteen grand. He had made a climb of about ten thousand feet—nearly two miles.

"I whiffed-out in cloud at fourteen-seven," said Bobo, suggesting that cloudbase was probably still that high. And so was my amigo. Oddly, I remembered that the only gloves Mauricio had were the ones stuffed in his helmet liner; his hands must be frozen and probably the rest of him too.

We all watched as that wing made slow progress across the threatening sky. As we watched, a bolt of lightening split the heavens. From our perspective, it was as though Mauricio flew right through it. But he was still up there, still poking along, and I was quite relieved that this particular adventure was nearly at end. Once Mauricio arrived in the sky over the cliffs above town he would be in familiar turf, so to speak.

The yellow wing started down from the clouds within easy glide of the beach. Mauricio had his own vocal cheering section as he let down. While still about a mile above us his tiny little daughter caught on to what was happening and pointed a finger at her hero once again.

"¡Papa volar!" she cried. "¡Papa volar!"

Papa did indeed volar. We all watched with anxious glee as Mauricio brought that Mark IV down to pattern altitude and turned final for the lakeside field. He had his approach lined up perfectly and dove down into ground effect.

It had been at least five years since Mauricio had landed on his feet—apparently he was a bit rusty. In any event my amigo neglected to drop his landing gear, but settled instead to the grassy turf with a gentle plunk on his chest

The Aguila had landed!

~~~~~~~~~~~~~~~~   ~~~~~~~~~~~~~

You might have thought it was Quetzalcóatl himself, who had returned in victory. With a roar of approval we all raced out to the field, Patricia showing us all just how a mom can run with a babe in arms. Mauricio struggled to his knees and shoved the helmet off his brow one last time as he saw us coming. He gathered his legs underneath him and stood up, still attached to the wing. He grinned and grimaced back at us as we approached and was soon in a familiar embrace, his wife in his arms and his little girl wrapped around his neck. He looked smiling at me over his wife's hug.

"Damn!" he said rubbing his hands on her back. "¡Mis manos are frozen!"

~~~~~~~~~~~~~~~~~~~~~~~~~~~~~~~~~~~~

On the ride of death, all the world is far from me
On the ride of death, it's the nearest to being free
--Song verse by Richard Thompson

~~~~~~~~~~~~~~~~   ~~~~~~~~~~~~~~~~~

Surviving Colimótl or,
Photographers Are Made, Not Born

It was a helluva long glide down from the heights. The gringo was just glad to be off the mountain and headed towards the safety that awaited him, well... somewhere far below. About eight-thousand feet below.

The sky was hazy down there, and a layer of cumulus clouds was forming between the flier and Mexico. He would need to hurry to get through that thermal layer before the whole world clouded-up. He pulled the nose down and poured on the speed.

He was gliding around the flanks of the imposing Fire Volcano of Colima—an amazing geological feature that he'd only laid eyes on but two days ago. Ever since that startling moment when they'd turned the corner on the highway up from the coast, and first glimpsed these massive geological heights, the two gringos had been obsessed with trying to huck themselves from the lofty summit.

Now, having moments ago succeeded in such a leap, the gringo wanted to gaze at the volcano as he floated by, but found it was just too scary... The flanks were made of smooth cinder-ash that was still smoking in spots. The steep sides were cut and eroded by vast slide areas that ended far below in horrible devastation, dotted with rocks that seemed to be about the size of houses. Each time the gringo inspected the sight below, he seemed to wander in that direction too, which would do him no good. It was a long glide after all—if he hoped to survive until lunch he'd better keep the wings level, hold that best-glide airspeed, pay attention.

He flew around the Fire Volcano, paying attention. Soon he could start to make out the ground below as just a dark and forbidding grayness that should have been welcoming. But clouds were forming down there and he had to find a hole through them. He dared not abbreviate his glide at all because he knew it was a long one, a long glide out to anywhere he really cared to land. They'd scoped that out the day before and decided the thing to do was glide all the way out to the giant high-tension power lines that stretched along the volcano's lower flanks, and follow them to safety in the first field they came to.

But it was going to be a long glide...

The gringo was tempted to dive for a convenient hole in the clouds, but he thought he might be able to glide over just one more cloud. That would take him out another quarter or half a mile towards safety.

If he could just get there...

Of course, if he didn't make it over the clouds, he would be forced to descend into the foggy mist and fly blind for as long as it took to pop out in the clear below. It seemed like a good bet though, so he prayed to the sky gods a bit, tried to hold his airspeed at best-glide, and just barely caught the edge of the next hole in the clouds. He banked the wing hard a starboard, pushed out to stall, and spiraled down into uncertainty.

When the gringo popped out at the base of the clouds, his bet had paid off. Now he was circling under a pleasant fair-weather cumulous cloud, which was being fed by gentle updrafts. He circled there, drifting slowly along at cloudbase, and getting his bearings.

Soon he spotted the power lines and whooped with relief—his drift was carrying him right along them and he thought he could actually see his landing field far beneath him. Some field was down there any way. Safety.

He circled there and enjoyed the sense of relief that came with knowing more-or-less where he was above the planet, and he hoped that Jake, who had launched just after him (or had he?), would show up to join him. But gradually the lift subsided and he began a last glide to Earth.

The field he aimed for was a large pasture on the furthest alluvial flanks of the volcano and he knew it sloped gently down towards the road. Soon he was setting up a landing for the *campo,* and he set himself up to land at the lower end. He swooped down into ground-effect and gradually let the nose up to bleed off speed. Then, with an all-mighty flare, he stood the wing on end and slammed on the air brake. He dropped the last few feet to Blessed Mexico, and let the wing settle gently onto his shoulders...

He had just survived a flight from fourteen thousand feet atop the Volcan de Fuego de Colima—Colimótl.

WahOOO!

He carried the wing to the shoulder of the paved road and plunked it down there. He quickly stripped off his harness and gear and folded it all carefully into his gear bag. He would start folding up the wing too, but first a moment to revel in his success... He reached into the wing and brought out a cold cervesa that he'd stashed there before launch, and from his shirt pocket he extracted a fat joint for his head. He popped the lid and sucked down the refreshing contents in a long draught, punctuated by a hearty belch. Then he fired up the doobie...

Life was BUENO!

At that moment he heard a vehicle approaching; it sounded like a wheezy beast and, sure enough, around the bend came a two-ton gate-bed International Harvester Loadstar, loaded from stem-to-stern with farm-worker types. The driver had just shifted into a higher gear when he spotted the grinning gringo standing in a field with a fancy wing the likes of he'd never seen before. Gringos standing in fields with hang gliders were just not a common sight here in the backcountry of central Mexico.

The load of peasants in the back of the truck, dressed in farm-worker gear, all waved at the gringo as they rolled past, and the driver began to ply the brakes. The engine downshifted through the gears, the brakes squealed in distress, and the Jake-brake hammered away. Finally, the farm wagon came to a noisy halt some distance beyond the unlikely spectacle. There came distinct gear-grinding sounds as the truck was double-clutched into reverse, and then it began slowly moving back towards the gringo, whining in protest. This made all the rear occupants very happy, and before long they had popped the pin on the rear gate that held them captive, swung a rear door open, and were climbing down to greet the gringo, and stand witness. All this, even as the truck continued to creep slowly backwards.

~~~~~~

Soon the whole show had stopped there in that beautiful pasture below that smoking volcano, one and all caught up in the spirit of flight.

The gringo didn't speak much Español and the peasants didn't speak much Ingles, but it didn't take long for the peasants to figure out what the stranger had done. He pointed to the lofty heights and then at himself. He held his arms out at his sides like a strange bird. He swooped this way and that, flapping like a dang fool...

"¡Volar!" he cried. "¡Volar!"

"¡Volar!" echoed the campesinos. "¡VOLAR!"

This was followed by a close inspection of the gringo, his gear and especially his wing. Everyone gazed up towards the towering heights, where the clouds had disappeared and the smoke had settled down.

"¿No le da miedo?" they asked. *Doesn't it scare you?*

Of course it scares me, thought the flier. Scares the be-Jeezus out of me at times. But most of the time it's just fun. That's why I do it. Now how to explain that in my poor Spanish?

"No señor," he lied. "No me da miedo."

That might have really impressed his new-found amigos, but they were worker-types; they were soon loading back into the Harvester, bent on scratching a living from the soil. The gringo grabbed one of them by the elbow and showed him his camera.

"Favor toma un foto señor," he pleaded. *Please take a picture sir.*

"¡Sí señor!" agreed the new amigo.

The gringo handed the campesino his Agfa compact 35mm aim-and-shoot. He pointed out the shutter button and pushed it once to demonstrate how to shoot. But when he stepped back to pose for the shot it became quite clear that the campesino really had no idea how to take a photo; he held the camera out at arm's length and tried to line up the shot, moving it this way and that...

So the gringo strode back to the campesino and gave him some simple directions.

"Ves la ventanita chiquita?" he asked. *See the little tiny window?*

"Síííí…"

"Ve la…" *Look through it…*

Campy peered through the tiny glass. "¡Ohhh!" he said, with sudden comprehension. "Ya lo ve." *Now I see.*

"Ahora," continued the airman. "El volcan atras, el camino abajo, el papalote al centro." *Now, the volcano behind, the road in front, the kite in the middle.*

"Bueno," said Campy. "Ya lo entiendo." *Okay, now I understand.*

The gringo hustled over to stand beside his wing while the Harvester fired suddenly to life and the gears ground into low. "Vamanos!" yelled the driver.

With studied care, Campy took a photo, likely the first ever of his life, and handed the gringo his camera. It had taken about three segundos.

"Adios amigo," he said with a limp handshake. "¡Vaya con Dios!" He began to run towards the truck. *Goodbye friend. Go with God!*

The Harvester was already rumbling off over the next hill as the campesino ran to catch up with his destiny. The gringo stood in the field with his camera in hand, waving at his departing amigos, who all waved a happy farewell in return.

He stood there hoping he had the shot for a moment or so, then started bagging his wing.

My Kingdom For A Vowel or,
Communication Breakdown #227

Dressed in ragged shorts and clean T-shirt Walter sat in the Palacio Gobierno, in the central Mexican city of Colima and admired the view. From the third story windows in the office of the Secretaria de Tourismo, he could look out over the jardine, over the tops of coconut palm trees swaying gracefully in the tropical breeze, and out across an enormous lush alluvial up to the magnificent vista of the Volcan de Fuego rising through the haze in the distance.

The Fire Volcano!

Snow capped and smoking, the view was always breathtaking and Walter remembered briefly his flight of survival, some years before, from that very same volcano. His pulse quickened at the sight, but not just at the sight of such great adventure...

His view was also smitten by a very fragrant Secretaria of Tourismo herself, who was seated across a large and spotless mahogany table, and who even now offered Walter some sugar for his tea. The appendage she extended to comply with the nod of his head was a delicious brown hand, slender and flawless, with perfectly manicured cherry-red painted nails.

Quite dumbfounded and awestruck, and somewhat tongue-tied as well, Walter tried not to stare, or even worse to drool, as he acquainted himself with the Secretaria de Tourismo for the Estado de Colima, not just another of the most stunningly beautiful of women that seemed to be everywhere here in Old Colima town. Tall and slender, clad in a shapely silk dress that showed magnificent décolletage, Maribel Ortiz de Mora was truly a spectacular creature. With skin the color of fancy-grade bee honey that just begged to be tasted, with cool green eyes that longed to be gazed into, and with raven-black hair piled atop her head to reveal a shapely neck, a neck that cried to be nuzzled, she smiled briefly at Walter and dispensed with formalities:

"¿Diga me señor Walter, que es su negocio aqui en Colima?" *Tell me Mr. Walter, what is your business here in Colima?*

Momentarily lost in her smile, Walter wondered how it would be to crush those labios in an impassioned embrace, to see leftover traces of her crimson lipstick in unnatural places... His imagination flashed upon the old crumbled and abandoned Hacienda Monte Rico he'd stumbled upon just the other day, hidden in the jungle under the flanks of yonder volcán. He had a sudden exquisite and unlikely vision of himself in only his birthday suit, running wild through the ruins, gleefully chasing the bare-naked Secretaria herself through the ancient papaya orchard in the moonlight... while she squealed in delight to let the gringo catch her from behind... to throw her roughly to the earth... to crush those luscious lips in hungry passion... to be her one-and-only tourista for one unforgettable noche... to have his way with such magnificence for just one heavenly night or possibly...

Por siempre jamás... *Forevermore!*

Mentally slapping himself on the kisser, he regained his senses and answered the simple question with the simple truth: "Soy guia señora," he replied. *I am a guide m'am.*

Powerful fragrance of orange blossoms washed through the open window, quaffed upon a gentle breeze from the lovely garden below the window.

A pink-and-blue butterfly fluttered by...

The Secretaria flashed her fiery eyes at the gringo and cleared her lovely throat.

"Señorita..." she intoned, to clarify the situation.

"Ah sí, sí, sí, por supuesto... ¡Señorita!" exclaimed Walter happily. "¡Desculpe!" *Excuse me!*

Here was a development with startling implications; Maribel Ortiz de Mora, Secretaria de Tourismo for the entire Estado de Colima (may I call you Cariña?) is not a Missus at all as Walter had assumed. She is apparently yet single, a MISS ... a señorita!

Available?

Furthermore, by inference, the single Mexican female is also...

Do you suppose...?

Virgin?

Nahhh!

Couldn't be!

Yet Walter found himself one step closer to that wild night of unforgettable lovemaking under the steaming volcano. He tingled with delight from head to toe and everywhere in between, was delighted with a burgeoning tumescence in his Bermudas.

Señorita Maribel Ortiz de Mora graced the gringo with another demure glance as she raised her china teacup to her lips. The pinkie she extended towards the gringo was delicate, like the stem of a fragile flower—the nail a bold red that matched her luscious lips. Clearly here was a woman in the prime of life and wearing it well. And speaking of wearing, that silk dress she was wearing would look best as a crumpled heap on the jungle floor.

Bueno!

Was that a sly smile?

Gently, she set down her teacup to continue.

"¿Y como eres usted guia aquí señor?" she inquired. *And how is it that you are a guide here sir?*

Walter had been bringing gringo glideheads to Colima for some time now and was in this office today to inquire if the Office of Tourism for the State of Colima might offer any help with his numerous problems, most notably; how to fund the construction of a new launch structure atop La Cumbre, a ramp to replace the rickety platform that currently clung to the cliffside. But in the face of the wonderful pulchritude seated across from him as they sipped tea and enjoyed the morning, such problems seemed just too mundane. Nothing less than eternal happiness—peace and plenty—sat just across the desk from the gringo. He might even stick his Teva-clad foot under the table and start a game of footsy if he was but a little bolder.

But Walter would have to pour on the charm now, if he ever hoped to see Señorita Maribel's shapely posterior running naked in the moonlight. He wished that he had spent a few more pesos on his business attire. He sat a bit straighter in his chair, sucked in his gut a bit more... As Señorita Maribel Ortiz de Mora lifted her teacup to moist red lips, Walter summoned his finest Mexican accento and gave his best repuesto:

"Tengo viejas por extranjeros," he declared happily. *I have old ladies for foreigners.*

The response was immediate from the señorita, but it was definitely NOT what Walter had been aiming for. Instead of nodding her head in approval at the gringo, she gagged on the tea as she sipped, and an unsightly froth of Earl Grey exited her shapely nose. A few drops were spilled down her silky breast and into her lap. She recovered quickly with a linen napkin over her mouth, and continued her inquiry "¿Viejas?" she gasped. *Old ladies?*

"Sí señorita," confirmed the gringo proudly. "Mis clients vienen aqui para vacacionar." *Yes Miss, my clients come here to vacation.*

What could be better than that, right?

But now she looked upon the gringo with eyes wide in disbelief.

"¿Viejas?" she inquired again. *Old ladies?*

Walter just nodded confidently and grinned foolishly... Then,

"¿Viejas señor, o viajes?" she asked with astonishment: *Old ladies... or trips?* The distinction was slight, but enormous as well! One silly vowel made all the difference.

Walter suddenly realized his mistake, saw his latest sexual fantasy collide with reality. If he ever hoped to get closer to Maribel Ortiz de Mora than across the immense expanse of her desk, he would need to think fast. Blushingly, he blundered on.

"Desculpe señorita, tengo mucho de aprender con este idioma," he stammered now: *Excuse me Miss, I have much to learn about this language.*

This was certainly true enough, if understated... And all might yet have been fine had the gringo just stopped there, just kept his big mouth shut for once. But no—he had to add one more bit of wisdom. Blundering on, he conjured up another word, a word he had overheard only yesterday while shopping in the mercado. He had been eavesdropping on a conversation between two other young lovelies when he heard it and it certainly seemed to fit the situation now:

"Estoy tan embarasado!" he declared. *I am so pregnant!*

Señorita Ortiz de Mora stood suddenly from her chair and wiped her blouse of a few stray spots of Earl Grey.

Pregnant?

The gringo is *pregnant?*

She looked away from Walter, as she explained that her subordinate spoke better "Ingles" and could Walter wait but a second? At that, she turned and strode through the entrance of her office, a provocative swaying in her shapely caboose. Walter heard a brief dialog, and then was relieved to see his fantasy female return to the office with yet another attractive woman in tow. This was Colima after all—the City of Shapely Señoritas. After brief introductions Walter was asked to state his case again—in English please!

He explained... that if he was to continue to bring gringos to Colima... to spend their gringo dolares... and to huck themselves off cliffs... he was going to need a new launch ramp. More importantly, he would need money for such a project.

For her part, Señorita Maribel Ortiz de Mora seemed only to want to end the meeting, which had been nothing if not brief, a few sentences in all... It was quickly agreed that she would look into the matter, she offered a cool hand to Walter in farewell, the meeting was suddenly terminated, and

Walter found himself back out on the street where he belonged.

It was only some months later when Walter came to understand how just badly he had screwed-up, there in that beautiful office, in that lovely city, with that gorgeous señorita:

¡Verguenza!

'Verguenza', is the word for shame or embarrassment, in Spanish. If Walter had simply said "¡Que verguenza!" *What shame!* all might have been fine and our hero might even now be enjoying marital favors from the loveliest flower in all of Colima. Who knows, might even have become the first gringo Señor of Tourismo in all of Mexico. Might have even had the chance to discover the real meaning of... *embarasado.*

Pregnant!

Such was the level of absurdity of Walter's life among the Mexicans. In this silly episode "I have trips for foreigners" became "I have old ladies for foreigners." And "I am so embarrassed" became "I am so pregnant."

Encounter With Dinner or,
This Little Piggy Went Wee Wee Wee!

The white sand beach of Bahia Tenacatita swept away in a giant arch, and as Walter walked home along the beach he reflected that all was wonderfully right with the world. The Pacific swells pounded the beach and set the ground to trembling. It would be a good day for bodysurfing. The sea breeze that set up every day was just now beginning to blow, and the frigate birds, giant prehistoric looking creatures, were already soaring the coconut palms that lined the bay. With a bit of luck, maybe there would be some ridge soaring for a gringo today, high above the idyllic scene.

Far down the beach, Walter could see Juanito and his trike, climbing out into the clear blue Mexican sky, hoisting yet another gringo off the beach and fleecing his wallet for some more of those precious pesos. *Keep up the good work Juan, thought Walter.*

He was returning from a morning walk into the village on the south end of the bay, a tiny fishing village called La Manzanilla, which Walter had only just learned means 'The Chamomile' in Español. The Chamomile is a sleepy burg where Walter liked to go for delicious huevos rancheros and a liquado for breakfast. In the evening, an old señora and her fragrant brown daughters would set up a dining room al fresco in the dusty street and serve delicious piles of pozole and warm stacks of tamales. Walter and Juan were regulars at both kitchens and his willingness to walk two miles down the beach for dinner had label Walter a "pozolero". It was a moniker the gringo wore with pride.

Today, as Walter walked down the beach, he realized that in the distance he could faintly hear, over the crashing surf, an agitated squealing coming from the enormous old abandoned hotel hidden in the palm grove. As he approached closer the reason for such a commotion became clear enough when he spotted a curious thing: from the jungle emerged a pig. An enormous sow pig maybe—though Walter couldn't be sure. An angry pig, in any event. This particular pig appeared to be lashed by means of a crude harness to a cumbersome bundle of some sort, and it was struggling against the burden while an old granny type—an abuela—accompanied the beast at some distance. As Walter looked on from afar while trudging along the beach, the old doña appeared to prod the pig with a pole. Whereby, the critter redoubled her efforts at escaping, and squealed some more.

Turning away from the water's edge, Walter walked up the sloping beach to investigate. As he did so he became aware that the old granny was the familiar figure of the "pozolera" tamale lady herself, and that the sow who was making all the noise was attached to an old fisherman's net filled with a couple hundred pounds of elotes—corn-on-the-cob—by means of a makeshift harness of old polyester rope. The señora held a ten-foot bamboo pole in her hands, from whose end protruded a rusty spike that was lashed to the pole, and with which she was busy prodding the poor creature down the beach.

With each jab in her haunches, the sow would squeal in protest and lurch her burden a few more meters towards the Chamomile. Blood oozed from several wounds on her haunches where the prod had already done its damage.

"Buenos dias señora," offered Walter as he neared the old woman. She acknowledged the gringo with a bit of a toothy smile that lasted just a fraction of a second, but otherwise she was all business, and hurried around the fishing net, carefully avoiding the angry beast, to prod it once more towards the distant village.

Walter let the woman pass, meanwhile keeping well clear of the pig. The beast looked as though he/she would like to trample and gore the nearest human who was not holding a prod, or who had any less resolve than his/her tormentor.

The gringo stood watching the strange march of the old señora and the angry captive pig. Then he noticed Toño, caretaker at the abandoned hotel. Toño stood watching the show too, grinning all the while. He waved at Walter from the cool shade of verdant green palm trees. The gringo walked up to greet Toño.

"¿Que pasa amigo?" he asked. *What's up?*

Toño grinned some more, pulled a wad of grubby pesos from the pocket of his trousers, and waved them at the visitor. "Vendi el cochino," he said. *I sold the pig.*

"¿Vendiste el cochino?" inquired Walter, pointing at the unlikely pair. *You sold that pig?* The gringo was new at this Español stuff, and was happy anytime he could hold a conversation, however simple.

"Sí," Toño grinned happily. "Mil pesos." *A thousand pesos.*

"Bueno..." confirmed Walter. "¿Y que pasa con los elotes?" he wondered aloud. *And what about those corn-on-the-cobs?*

"Elotes tambien," explained Toño proudly. *The corn too.* "Se compro el cochino y todo los elotes que se puede jalar." Walter had to mull this bit of info over a few times... *She bought the pig and all the corn it could haul.*

Walter and Toño stood on the beach under the palms and watched the drama unfold as the sea breeze washed over them. The captive cochino and the old tamale granny slowly made their tortured way towards the village, a crazy dance of survival, in what must have been an ancient journey to the market.

This little piggy went "wee wee wee" all the way home.

A couple of near-naked children dashed out from their huts on the beach when they heard the beast squealing, and hit it with a stick, urging it along, we may suppose, to its destiny. Two bold seagulls tried to steal a couple kernels of corn, but the old woman swung at them with her prod. She had a swing like Tigers slugger Rocky Colavito.

And the gringo came to understand that he would soon become even more familiar with the tasty pig, and its savory burden too.

Circling Disease or,
Therapy—Old Mexico Style

Walter had circling disease all right, that much was diagnosed more than twenty-five years earlier. Even after a quarter-century of treatment the diagnosis was still the same: acute circling disease. That particular malady is brought on by gentle breezes and high cloudbases, and aggravated by pocket thermals* and safety meetings*. Mountains didn't help the problem either, they simply intensified the itch. The prognosis was: possibly terminal. The only wintertime therapy thus far known to man, or to that man anyway, was to drive deep into Mexico, find a cliff somewhere, and throw himself off.

You see what they mean by 'terminal'.

This sort of activity was just plain dangerous, even for a young man. But Walter was a beat-up old glidehead, who just didn't have the sense enough to stand around on the ground forever, and figure his circling days were done. Nope, the only possible cure, or even temporary treatment, was lots more circles.

~卪≥≤卪~

He picked up the wing and steadied it in the breeze. A bead of sweat dribbled off his brow onto his glasses and ran down the inside of the left lens. A gust lifted one wing dramatically and he was forced to set it all back down. The thermal seemed

---

pocket thermal- marijuana cigarette (you keep it in your pocket, it get's you high) also: joint, reefer, hooter, fattie, doobie
safety meeting- a bunch of people smoking the above marijuana cigarette (See Tales From The Wild Blue Yonder RECIPES FOR DISASTER for more info)

~~~~~~~~~~~~~~~~~~~~~~~~~~~~~~~~~~~~~~~

to be building however, so he picked it right back up, level now.

He saw the streamer on the hillside below line up with his nose and he felt the wing suddenly lighten... it tugged gently forward... it wanted to fly... Leaning through the control bar Walter took three giant steps towards the edge, three giant steps towards uncertainty. He held the nose down as he ran, and shoved off with his toe—one more step. The glider cut a beautiful clean arch away from the hill.

It was time for some therapy!

~ 🔃 ≥ ≤ 🔃 ~

The Mexican had popped his head over the wing about an hour earlier as Walter was stuffing battens. He grinned at Walter and said,

"¿Usted va a volar?" *Are you going to fly?*

It wasn't the brightest of questions under normal circumstances, but one that could not now be answered with a straight "yes" or "no". How to explain to someone who's probably never seen a hang glider, never met anyone with acute Circling disease, who sees you stuffing battens into a funny-looking orange wing and figures he's here just in time to see you jump? How to explain, especially if you must do the explaining in a foreign tongue?

"Yes," was not at all a certainty. In fact, if the conditions didn't look any better than the last attempt just yesterday, then maybe "no" was more certain. Desperate though he was, Walter had no desire to repeat yesterday's performance of sinking out into the Hell of the valley below with hardly a circle to speak of, where he'd skinned his knee on landing. This was just not therapeutic at all. To make matters worse, to add insult to injury, a few stinkin' parabags had launched ahead of the gringo and skyed-out, getting plenty of circling therapy and turning into happy little dots overhead. Nope. The glider could always be put BACK in the bag.

Instead, he changed the subject: "Veniste a pie?" he asked. *Did you come here on foot?*

The Mexican nodded and grinned some more. This, in spite of the fact that he had just climbed a steep mountain trail up a thousand vertical feet at least, in blazing sun and heat, without so much as a bottle of water in evidence, or a drop of sweat for that matter. Dressed in a flannel shirt and trousers and boots like a logger, he still looked fresh. How do they do it, the Mexicans?

Walter was bathed in sweat, even though he had driven to the top in his Ford and was setting up in the shade cast by a giant statute of the Virgen* of Guadalupe. Just spreading wings and stuffing battens and pulling tension was all it took in such tropical heat, for the gringo to break a sweat. A drop dripped into his eye and stung him blind.

"Si señor," the Mexican answered, and then asked again, "¿Va volar usted?" *You gonna fly?*

Walter figured he owed the guy a straight answer, the only question was: which one? So he said the only thing that made sense;

"Tal vez." *Maybe.*

There might have been a touch of desperation in his voice but of course, the Mexican couldn't know that. Walter was indeed desperate to fly, the flying had sucked for three stinkin' days now—very high pressure over an inverted sky. Circles were desperately needed. No less than a hundred circles

~~~~~~
Virgen- in Mexican Spanish you pronounce it "BEER-hen"

would do the job, but the more the better...

He turned his attention to the wing, not to be anti-social or even unfriendly to the Mexican, but just because it was so damned hot, hotter than Hades, and you just had to keep moving, get set up, and get off. There was no energy for polite small talk. But the Mexican seemed satisfied with a "tal vez", *maybe*, and disappeared around the corner of the imposing cathedral that was perched on launch. The gringo put the finishing touches on the wing and took a gulp of water. *Gotta stay hydrated*, he thought.

Soon, in spite of the conditions, Walter's glider was all set up and waiting, the flight-deck was mounted to the base tube, the harness and helmet laid out at the ready. Nothing more to do now but to check the conditions at launch. He rounded the corner of the cathedral and hobbled over to launch, trying not to limp too obviously. The flags at launch hung depressingly flat, wafted now and then by a stray puff, but very weak and inconsistent. As Walter watched, a pathetic cycle came up the hill and got them flapping, stood them up for a few seconds. The cycle provided no relief from the heat however; in fact launch was a fiery hell, hotter than blazes. Even the myriad local buzzards were just perched on the radio towers, gazing down as though watching the gringo for some action.

Below, a few paragliders who had launched while he was making ready, set up approaches to the fields in the valley. Even they had stunk-out today and Walter had no desire to join them. He turned disgustedly away from launch, cursing the high pressure, and sought shelter in the shade. As he did there was a call from above.

"HowEEEE!" he heard.

He looked up to the statute of the Virgen de Guadalupe standing atop the cathedral standing atop the summit, and there was the Mexican. He had scaled to the roof of the church, climbed the onion-dome itself, and then crawled up the Virgen's gown. Now he poked his head out a tiny window in her knees.

"¡YahOOO!" he hollered again. "¡WOOOHOOE!" He grinned down upon the gringo from fifty feet above, and threw out his arms as though he too might fly. "¿Vas a volar?" he cried from his lofty perch. Directly above his head a small windsock on an antenna puffed weakly in the smothering heat. "¡Brincate!" he urged. "¡Salte! ¡Andale!"

JUMP!

LEAP!

DO IT!

Walter reached the shade and took a load off. He plunked his sorry ass down in the deepest part of the shade there atop the summit, and was grateful for it. He tried to make a decision.

Fly it?

Bag it?

Let's not and say we did it?

He looked at his watch: 1:45. *I'll give it thirty minutes to turn on and then I'll take a look*, he determined. *If the day has not improved I will bag it.* That was the most commitment he could give the day. The temptation was to bag it, but that would mean four days without circling therapy.

Bad.

A thermal rustled through launch. He heard it whistling through the windows of the cathedral and around the concrete figure of the Virgen. It was enough to coax the gringo out from under his rock and back to launch for a moment. This was no thermal to write home about, but it was a cycle. Walter watched it straighten-up the streamers for a moment and checked his watch again: 2:07. Eight minutes until decision time.

He walked back to his wing and there stood the Mexican again. He had descended from his heavenly perch to walk about like other sensible mortals. But he spread his arms like silly wings, and flapped them like a bird. He swooped and swirled a hand and made whooshing flying sounds.

"¡Uuuhhhooo!" he intoned. "¿Como lo siente señor?" *How does it feel?* "¿Para que esperas señor?" *What are you waiting for gringo?* and "¡Brincate!"

JUMP!

"Fudge!" muttered Walter. "Shoot!" Urged on by the Mexican, he stood and began suiting-up. It was not a lengthy process in this heat; a sweatshirt and light gloves were the whole flying get-up. He pulled the harness over his head and sweat flowed over his glasses, effectively blinding him. Sunscreen flowed into his eyes, making them sting even worse. He took off his glasses and wiped them clean with a shirttail. He wiped the slop off his face. He hobbled over to the wing and clipped in. He pulled the helmet over his head and put on the glasses—first his weak readers, then his sunglasses. For better or worse- he was ready. He shouldered the glider and moved to launch. The Mexican hovered nearby.

"¡Brincate!" he yelled. "¡Brincate!"

~ᴎ≥≤ᴎ~

Walter waited patiently on the cycle. He'd had a good, strong launch. He was immediately rewarded with seven circles. Seven circles took him to about three hundred feet—not nearly enough therapy. He began to sink then, and was forced to point the glider towards the hellish valley below. He glided out and begged the Sky Gods for any little morsel of lift to circle in.

"I promise!" he prayed. "I promise I'll stick with it like glue! I won't leave until I top-out! Te lo juro!" *I swear!*

Walter sunk.

Then he sunk some more.

He followed the saddle out from launch and tears of frustrating anxiety welled up behind his glasses. He was horribly sick with disappointment. The valley was only one desperate turn away when the glider stopped sinking. Walter checked his altitude and made a hesitant turn. He completed the circle and checked his altitude again; he had lost three feet. He made another circle and lost another three feet. He adjusted the circle a bit this time, moving slightly away from the valley and in towards the rocky, cactus-covered hillside. His vario sung to life with a sweet beeping and he re-checked his altitude; this time, he had gained three feet.

He circled to more happy beeps.

He was climbing, however painfully slowly—about three feet a circle. But he was climbing.

And circling.

And suddenly...feeling good!

Now the thermal came to life and moments later he was back at launch-level. Gripped on the bar now, he could see the Mexican standing there at launch, exhorting him, with what words Walter could only guess. He circled some more and the Mexican got smaller. The radio towers swung past on the way up, now to twenty-five hundred feet, then twenty-six hundred. Now the lift really turned on and Walter circled, feeling much better with each turn. He was well above the Virgin now, and climbing... circling... Apparently, she had answered his prayers.

Below him, the Mexican looked like a tiny ant, a demented ant, an ant who danced crazily about the mountaintop with his arms out like a silly pajaro—a flying ant maybe. Circling and drifting, the glider crested La Cumbre and the lift became solid. Occasional glances at the altimeter showed steady results—three grand, then thirty-five-hundred, then four grand, where it suddenly shut off. About thirty circles had been made.

Craving more, Walter pointed the glider out the side of the ridge towards home. He slowed once for a false alarm, a teaser, and then continued gliding, gliding, sinking towards the fields at La Caseta.

Not La Caseta...! A worse place to land and bag the glider could not be imagined.

Por favor not La Caseta!

More than half-way there the vario beeped into life again. Just a marginal thermal coming up out of a cañon below, but large enough to circle in.

Walter circled.

And prayed.

Please God! Anything! Just give me another grand! I'll take ANYTHING!

On the next circle the vario beeped encouragingly all the way around. The net gain was better than fifty feet. Walter circled. A red-tail hawk jumped into the thermal below, and then a whole family of buzzards joined in too. Suddenly, Walter had himself a party and everyone was getting good circling therapy.

He grinned.

He drooled a little.

He circled some more and hit pay-dirt as he cranked and banked—a powerful column of air was flowing up from the canyon below and headed for the Heavens. On the way up he shouted for joy.

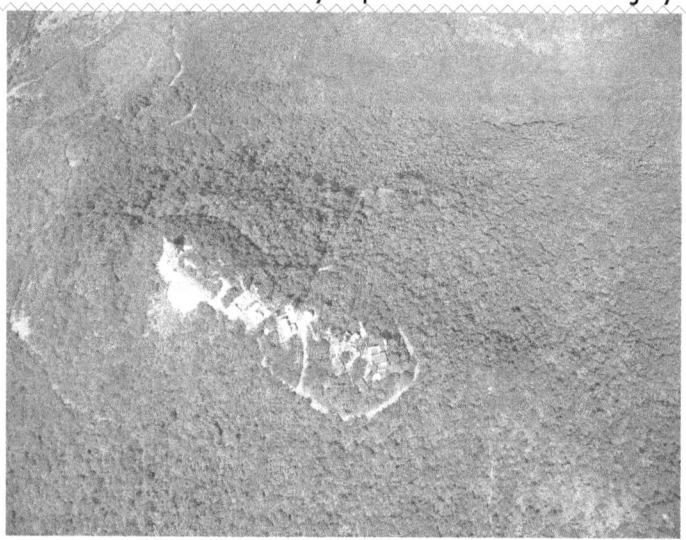

The BEER-hen is down there. See her?

"I feel GREAT!" he cried to nobody, to the buzzards, to the Sky Gods above and the BEER-hen below. To the Mexican who had exhorted him into action.

"¡YO SIENTO CHINGON!"

Several hundred circles later, having climbed to seven thousand feet over old Colima town and flown home to a gentle landing, Walter felt complete, yet again. The Circling Disease was in remission.

Our Lady Of The Sorrows Revisited or, Day Of The Slobs

Mexico has many lengends. One legend has it that the original Mexica tribe had a shaman who insisted that they depart their ancestral homeland on the Ancient Island City of the Pendejos, and wander about until they beheld an eagle, sitting in a cactus, with a serpent in its claws. That is why the Mexican flag even today bears this symbol.

Legend also has it that a lovely virgin appeared before a simple peasant more than four centuries ago and, to make a long story short, became known as Our Lady of the Sorrows, La Morenita, and the Virgin of Guadalupe—the patron Saint for all of Mexico.

The following tale is a modern update of those events—legend revisited.

~~~~~~~~~~~~~~~~~~~~~~~~   ~~~~~~~~~~~~~~~~

Mexico, a land where even the agnostics are Catholic.
-Carlos Fuentes

I n his hotel room, Walter tossed and turned and sweated. Down the street the cantina was in full swing, pumping out Mexican polkas and rancheros at a torturous volume. The bass woofer thumped to the point of quake-like vibrations and cars roared in and out of the parking lot, up and down the street. Other sounds of Mexico tormented the gringo as well, jake-brakes, topes, and trucks roaring into the humid night. Dogs barking at nothing. Even roosters crowing at midnight. But the gringo was quite exhausted from the day's crazy events and so he shoved some of those little foam earplugs in his ears, pulled a pillow over his head, and turned the overhead fan on 'high' to provide some white-noise relief. Some time after midnight, he finally fell into a fitful sleep... and dreamed...

He tossed...
He turned...
And he dreamed...

ﬦ≥≤ﬦ

Nearly five centuries ago, on the chilly morning of December 9, 1531, he was crossing the barren hill called Tepeyac, hurrying to go fling himself from the Rock of the Devil. He was brought to a sudden halt by a blinding light and the sound of a Mexican polka called Chinga Tu Madre, blaring so loudly it was distorted beyond all comprehension. Suddenly, before him appeared a gaudy vision; a beautiful foxy chica—a morenita—who, calling the gringo 'Guero' (Whitey) declared herself to be the Virgin (sic) Mary herself, the mother of none other than Jesus H. Christ himself. As she shimmered there before him, this unlikely vision explained to Walter that it was her desire to have an enormous pile of reeking trash and stinking garbage dumped atop Tepeyac hill, and everywhere else in Mexico for that matter, and asked him to relay this message to Bishop Juan de Zumarraga de la Pendeja y Subuey in old Colima town.

It was no easy task for the pagan norteño to be granted an audience with the top Bible thumper, but the persistent gringo was finally admitted to the inner sanctum. The incredulous Bishop didn't believe the gringo's loco story for a minute, and demanded that he be provided with some proof of the alleged encounter, but of course the gringo had none and so he departed forthwith.

Somewhat relieved and quite indifferent to the so-called 'virgin' and her request anyway, Walter went flying for several days. But on December 12, while rushing to get to launch early because the Heavens were popping full of cumulous clouds, he took a shortcut up the hill. The Virgin once again appeared, this time to the tune of No Te Metes Con Mi Cucu, and as he continued stuffing battens, Walter told her that the Bishop was having none of it—he was busy molesting young boys anyway—he had no interest in a mamacita, virgin or not.

The Virgin instructed the flier to gather an armload of stinking trash from the beach and from the Camino Real, and deliver it summarily to Juan

Zumarraga de la Pendeja y Subuey as a sign— garbage the fouler the better.

The dream was becoming a bit of a pesadilla then, as Walter gathered up some reeking and disgusting trash where previously there had been none and, carrying it in his helmet, hurried off to complete his mission.

Once again before the Bishop, he let the garbage spill out before him and lo and behold, it was a road-kill dog, sitting on the remains of a busted piñata and holding a dirty disposable diaper in his jaws.

To the wonder of all assembled, and for reasons that the gringo will never understand, a perfect image of Gloria Esteban herself was revealed emblazoned on Walter's chest. And so it came to pass that, to this very day, a dead dog, sitting on a pile of dirty diapers and holding a tattered old piñata in his jaws, remains the símbolo nacional de México...

~ଯ≥≤ଯ~

Walter awoke shaken and sweaty from his horrible nightmare, and knew what he had to do. It had come to him in the night like an unholy vision and there was no pinche cabron pendejo buey who was going to stop him now.

He scrambled into his shorts and sandals and was pulling on his tee shirt even as he blew out his hotel door. He sprinted across the lobby and out the salida and down the block to the OXXO (convenience store), and around to the side of the building where there was no shortage of trash. He startled a few starving dogs who were scrounging for a breakfast amongst the Pinguino and Choco Rolles wrappers, and quickly spotted what he was after. He grabbed an empty Pampers box—the largest piece of cardboard he could find—and cut out one big panel. Then he hurried home where we took his biggest Magic Marker in hand and carefully outlined the following words in large block letters:

NUESTRO SEÑORA DE LA BASURA
(OUR LADY OF THE TRASH)

It was December 13, the day after (of course) December 12—Dia de la Virgen de Guadalupe—which is the one single day every year when the pious catholic 'peregrinos' go up to the chapel atop launch on La Cumbre and completely trash the place in a religious fervor. Walter was devastated to discover that La Cumbre, a place he held quite sacred himself through the years, a place that to himself and many other flyers is quite literally the Stairway to Heaven, a power spot, a place where he could and did blast into the sky, a place that he loved so much that he would drive thousands of miles on a pilgrimage of his own every year just to stand at the edge and leap...

La Cumbre had become a foul wasteland of cochino Mexican indifference and religious mierda.

On December 12 every year, ten thousand or more Colimencese and Jalisciences and chilangos and pendejos Mexicanos from all over the country, would scale the mountain on a pilgrimage to the crude iconic statute of the virgin (sic) herself up there, and of course they brought along all sorts of silly icons and food and snacks and beverages and all manner of consumer goods which they consumed, and then dropped the trash where ever they stood, where ever it happened to fall, without regard for the other guy or common human decency whatsoever. Plastic cups, plates, forks and spoons dotted the landscape—and not one trashcan in evidence.

Numerous retail vendors took advantage of the situation too of course, so that here was a pile of watermelon rind and there a pile of orange peels and over there the remains of a 'carnitas', all of it gathering flies and reeking under the tropical sun. But nothing reeked quite so badly as the numerous piles of human shit, fecal matter—turds decorated by toilet paper—which speckled the landscape here and there.

Walter was filled with despair as he walked about among the refuse, careful not to step in shit.

He was too sick even to set up and fly. Where could he set up and not risk getting Hepatitis B? Cholera? Typhoid?

It was so disgusting!

How could they do this? To their own sacred site?

The Mexicans had climbed to their holy shrine, on its holy day, and they had shit upon it, figuratively and quite literally too. As he stood atop the launch ramp, a rippin' cycle roared through, snatched at a plastic plate, and sent it soaring upward, doing a demented dance on a diminutive dust devil. Walter watched it turn into a tiny spec as it climbed towards a cumulous cloud that appeared in the Heavens... The flier kicked out savagely at the nearest plastic cup and sent it flying off the edge.

Was even God a litterbug?

Was it Providential indifference?

Was it just plain ol' Ignorance rearing his ugly head?

It was this unhealthy vision that had spawned Walter's pesadilla, which had awakened him cold and sweaty.

Well, this time he wasn't lettin' them sanctimonious cochino bastards get off so chingada goddamn facilmente.

He would let them *know,* that the trash atop La Cumbre was not forgotten the moment it hit the ground.

He would let them *know,* that here was one gringo who was not about to tiptoe around their reeking shit every day when he went up to La Cumbre to fly.

He would make good and sure that they *know* there was one gringo who saw them as a bunch of swine.

He grabbed a piece of broken downtube and a roll of duct tape and fastened his sign to the tube as a handle. Then he jumped on his bicicleta and raced uptown and into the jardine central to the very door of God's kitschy castillo itself—the iglesia—the Catholic Church. Much as Juan Diego himself had done some 460 years earlier, he would flush the chingada padre out of his garish templo, and lay it on him straight. This time the old man would be confronted by no peasant with an armload of roses; this time the padre would see before him the very ugly Truth. And a pissed-off gringo.

Walter pumped the bike as fast as it would go, turned the corner into the jardin central, and skidded to a stop in front of the church doors. He was nervous to see that a large crowd had gathered there for some reason, and was wipping into some sort of religious fervor. He jumped off the bike and started waving his sign.

"Cochinos!" he yelled. "COCHINOS!" *Pigs! Pigs!*

The crowd was almost as startled to see the big gringo waving his sign as the gringo was desperate about his protest. All in all, these were very polite folks, just horrible litterbugs is all, which, as Walter saw it, was about the worst insult you could give someone. He was also surprised to see the Bishop himself, or a padre maybe, well anyway, some zealot in funny clothes and holding a tacky icon over the crowd, was standing right before him and giving the pagan his full attention.

"¿Cochinos?" he said to Walter. *Pigs?* His forehead creased with a frown and Walter could watch him read the protest sign:

NUESTRO SEÑORA DE LA BASURA

At that, Padre's demeanor changed abruptly. Wearing a frown now, he took two quick steps toward the intruder and swiped his hand at the sign. Walter towered over him however, he stood on tiptoes to foil the padre, and when he grabbed Walter's right arm the gringo moved his sign to the left. At such close quarters Walter could smell the old freak's body odor—a disturbing realization.

The scuffle did not last long though, because from behind the padre came the biggest, most imposing Mexican Walter had ever seen. The man was a *gigante* and he was quite obese as well. He had some strange disease or other condition that made him look a bit like a swarthy Fabulous Hulk from the neck up, a fat Wimpy from the neck down. To Walter, no small gringo himself, this freak looked to be about seven feet tall. The freak gently but firmly set the padre aside and took another step forward pinning Walter's foot to the ground with his own giant appendage, and he kept it there with his considerable weight.

Walter was immobilized with pain and stuck in position—suddenly he could not move. It was an easy task for the gigante to grab Walter's wrist and wrest the sign from his grip. Immediately, he crushed the cardboard between his paws, gave the gringo a look that said, *You're next!* and turned his back on the scene. He took a few steps towards the church and disappeared among the Catholics, many of whom were still wondering what had come to pass.

The padre stood his ground and said, "¿Que quiere usted, señor?" *What to you want, sir?*

"Que alguien limpie del despegue," replied the flier. *That someone go clean the launch.*

"¿Despegue?" questioned the priest. "¿Como que despegue?" *Launch? What do you mean 'launch'?*

"Usted sabe padre," replied the gringo. *You know what I mean father.*

The old man just looked at the gringo and shook his head, mystified. "Dios te bendigo," he insisted piously. *God bless you.*

"No quiero ningun bendigo de nadie," Walter said. *I don't want any blessing from anyone.* "¡Quiero que los cochinos limpian sus cochinadas!" *I just want the pigs to clean up their pigmess!*

"¿Que cochinada?" asked the padre. "*What pigmess?*"

Walter clutched the padre by his elbow, grabbing a handful of the voluminous folds of robe he was wearing, and dragged him a half-dozen paces to larboard. From there, they could just barely see La Cumbre in the distance, the site of the pigmess, with the iconic statute of the Virgen standing atop.

"¡Aquel cochinada!" he said while pointing. *That pigmess!*

The Padre was not happy about having been dragged against his will even the few steps they had taken, and he wrenched his arm away from the gringo without ever paying heed to where Walter pointed. Even less happy was Lurch, the imposing Mexican who—it suddenly became clear—was the old man's bodyguard. *Derepente*, he was standing behind the gringo and Walter felt his hand clutch into his neck from behind. Lurch applied pressure from his massive hand, and suddenly Walter was powerless. He marched the gringo like a helpless marionette to the corner of the church, pointed him away from the ceremonies, and gave him a shove.

Walter stumbled and turned and looked back and Lurch held his ground. In a pointed manner, he wiped his hands together a few times as though dusting the gringo off. *Good riddance to bad rubbish.*

It seemed likely that Walter's sign had been disposed of properly—at least it had found its way into a trash can. Now the gringo himself had been disposed of—white trash, pagan, never once accepting Jeezes H Christ as his savior—doomed to spend eternity in Hell. But there would be no more trouble for the faithful of Colima on this December 13. There was little else Walter could do but jump on his bici and beat an angry retreat.

Good riddance to bad rubbish!

~ⵍ≥≤ⵍ~

Once again atop La Cumbre, Benigno told the gringo, "No te preocupes nada." *Don't you worry none.*

It was the following Sunday and the local fliers had gathered for some heavenly fun, and so they were back on launch and 'Benny', one of the faithful La Cumbre fliers, had ordered his wife and young hijo to get busy cleaning up the cochinada. He had dispensed a rake and a shovel and ordered them to hustle-up. The flying was going to be great in an hour or two, so while Benny set up his wing and laid out his harness and gear, he would see to it that his loved-ones stayed busy.

They did not look too happy about the situation though, perhaps they blamed the gringo for their trouble. But neither one of them could deny the hombre of the familia; the hefe. They soon got to work in the hot sun.

Walter joined them too, grabbing a broom he kept in the Ford-From-Hell and sweeping the trash into piles. Little Benny—Benigno's son—was given the shovel and told to heave all the shit and the rotten garbage off the side of the mountain, either over the cliff or into the jungle, while Flora the wife and Walter the gringo, swept and raked everything that might burn into a dozen piles.

Then Benny poured gasoline on all the heaps of trash. He sucked on a Marlboro and threw the butt on the first pile. As all the faithful watched, the trash turned into heavy black smoke, which rose reluctantly into the heavens.

Tropico De Cancer or,
Wrong Way Gringo

Motoring up the coast highway from Guatemala to Arizona gave Walter plenty of time to reflect on his past, and to ponder his future. Sometimes he felt as though he was the luckiest gringo on the planet. Nothing to do all day but fly, fly and fly some more, with a bit of gluttony and debauchery thrown in at night to keep things interesting and satisfying.

There were other times when he just felt alone and empty. Like now, for example. The road from Central America to Phoenix, Arizona and beyond was just too hard and too long to go it alone. Left with only some rock 'n roll cassettes and his own thoughts for company, often he wished he hadn't fucked things up so badly with Tanya, wished he'd never met Trish, and was just plain confused by how fast his fire for Esmeralda had been doused...

¡Esmeralda!

~~~~~~~~~~~~~~~~   ~~~~~~~~~~~~~~~~

With a name like that she'd had to be outrageous. Maybe if he had been born a Napoleón or... or a Candíde... he might have lived up to, or even thrived on, her saucy character. As Walter the Gringo, he was just glad to be rid of her.

Wasn't he?

Oh, he would miss her satiny thighs and her bodacious ta-tas. The way she wagged them in his face when she wanted to tease him. He missed that warm pot of honey she was sitting on, her midnight ardor, and the way she smelled at dawn—a musty heaven that never failed to stir him to further ecstasy. But she was just so... loco! Maybe he should turn around, drive back deep into Mexico, find Esme again and confess, once again, his undying, everlasting, love and devotion...?

Of course, about eight hours up ahead lay Guaymas town...

And Lucy.

Didn't she just have a cumpleaños?

What would that make her?

Old enough probably...

A PEMEX station and a ramshackle cluster of buildings and huts hove into view through the last rays of sunset—two stations actually—one on each side of the highway, and startled him out of his self-pity and sorrowful speculation. He glanced at his gas gauge and saw it getting low. He'd better fuel up, stretch the weary bones, let Sarge out to piss.

Without slowing, he sped on past the stations for a kilometer or so, then braked and swung around and returned to the pumps. It was a ploy he used to deceive any banditos who may be lurking at the station, gunning for a weary solo traveler on the highway; they would think he was headed south.

Then, when he returned to the highway, he would drive out of town the wrong direction, in this case south for a ways, and then do a U-turn to see if he was being followed. It had saved his hide once or twice he was positive. A solo traveler was a big temptation to the Mexican highwaymen bandito cabrones.

He pulled up to the pump and was immediately set upon by a small boy—a chavo—with a wad of grubby oily rags in hand. Walter wagged his finger angrily at the child but he knew it was pointless. The kid was determined to rub that greasy rag on Walter's windshield, making it so filthy dirty as to be dangerous, in hopes that the gringo would be grateful enough to cut loose with a few pesos. Or even better yet—a gringo dólar. Walter would have to get out his Windex and paper towels and clean up the mess himself. He had no problem with the child's willingness or his industriousness. Nor was he indifferent to the urgency he must have felt to make a peso. Only his equipment was bad.

If the kid could actually provide a reasonable service, Walter would gladly pay the peso or two that was expected in return. But that would never happen. Without fail, the windshield would be left in worse shape that before.

The child had already climbed up on the bumper and sprayed the windshield with water, so when Walter stepped out of the Ford-From-Hell and stretched, he told the child: "¡No te pago!" *I won't pay you!* That stopped the chavo in his tracks.

"Yo limpio el vidrio, Señor," he implored the gringo. *I'll clean your window sir.*

~~~~~~~~~~~~~~~~ ~~~~~~~~~~~~~~~~

Walter grabbed the wretched urchin by the wrist and wrenched the rotten rag away from the child. "¡Es sucio!" he said irritably, holding the rag at arm's length. *It's filthy!*

The child appeared surprised that the gringo had taken his grimy bundle. It wasn't even a rag Walter noticed, it was some sort of cotton wadding gauze the likes of which Walter'd never even seen before, and it was so filthy it was like a bad joke. The child looked sheepishly at the traveler, as though he had understood all along. He was a determined sprout though; he held out his palm for a handout.

"¿Me regalas un peso, señor?" he pleaded. *Give me a peso sir?*

It was like this in every chingada gasolinera on the major chingada highways in all of chingada Mexico. Walter had seen hundreds of children the likes of this tyke, and become indifferent to them. There was just no way to help them all, even if he'd wanted to. So Walter got busy fueling. He unlocked the fuel door and then popped the hood on the Ford while the attendant began pumping fuel.

"Señor..." said the child again. He tapped Walter's leg and repeated his miserable mantra: "¿Me prestas un peso?" *Lend me a peso?* The child was not one to give up so easily. His demeanor had changed abruptly—now he was the pathetic victim of neglect.

"¿Donde vas?" asked the attendant as he pumped the gas. *Where are you going?* He looked over the truck carefully, noticing that Walter was a loner.

"Mazatlan," lied the gringo. Mazatlan was about two hours south of his present position—he'd left

Mazatlan behind two hours ago. Walter had passed a battered road sign that said TROPICO DE CANCER about two hours ago as he left the town of Mazatlan behind. He had slammed on the brakes and stopped to take a leak and a photo of the sign. He'd cracked a beer and put on some Bob Seger and continued on. Walter was NOT headed for Mazatlan now, but north, for Culiacan, Los Mochis, Guaymas and Nogales. For the States, for Gringolandia, for the Big PX—north, for the high country, with maybe a quick stop for Lucy. Summer was around the bend after all. He was headed for cool high country around Lake Tahoe. It just *looked* like he was traveling south because... Because he was a savvy traveler that's why.

¡Sabio!

"Mazatlan..." confirmed the attendant with a nod. Then, "¿Solo?" he asked. *Alone?*

Of course he was alone. He'd been alone since Guatemala fer Chris'sake, and it was a bit hellish. Anyone could see he had no company.

"¿Solo señor?" asked the attendant again.

"¡No!" He lied some more. "Voy con mi buen compañero." *I go with my good friend.*

The attendant looked confused at that. He'd seen no amigo in the truck. There was no one inside but Bob Seger, wailing away about a ramblin' gamblin' man.

"¿Compañero?" he asked. "¿Que compañero?" *What friend?*

Walter pointed into the back of the Ford, under where the gliders were all neatly tucked into the rack. There, lashed to an upright, was a cheap clay figure of Jesus H. Cristo Himself, who stood about three feet tall. He was a very gaudy, painted-up

Jesus in his robes and sandals, a Jesus with a tortured look upon his face, a Jesus holding his heart out in front of his chest as though he'd torn it asunder his own self, the aorta and ventricular a ghastly lavender spectacle. Walter had won the gruesome figurine at a carnival some months back—throwing baseballs at bowling pins. Who could come up with such a macabre spectacle, and then sell it to a carnival?

What nut-case?

What fool?

What... *pendejo?*

"¡Tengo amigo en Jesus!" exclaimed the gringo. *I have a friend in Jesus!*

It never hurt to let them think you were slightly *loco*.

Meanwhile, the child continued tugging on Walter's pant leg, palm outstretched, face pleading.

"¡Por favor, señor!" he begged.

The gringo was about ready to smack the kid but... A taco stand set up over near the edge of the crumbling parking lot was emitting a savory aroma, a smoky cloud of beef, onions and cilantro. It was close enough to the highway, and the blast of wind from passing traffic, that Walter knew the food would be slightly gritty at best and slightly toxic at worst, with a faint taste of diesel exhaust. But the aroma stirred his hunger, made his belly growl.

"¿Que te vas a comprar con un peso?" he asked the chavo, even though he knew the answer. *What will you buy with a peso?*

"Un dulce," confessed the child. *A sweet.*

Just what you need, Walter thought. He gestured towards the nearby taco cart. An old señora, with a piece of cardboard trash in hand, was fanning the flames from the small wood fire, and smoke curled up around her face. The ubiquitous dangling piece of raw meat hung on a hook nearby, flies buzzing around it. Even so, Walter knew the tacos would be tasty. This was the Land of Tacos after all.

"Vamos por unos tacos," he offered the child. *Let's go have some tacos.*

The boy quickly agreed. His face brightened and he smiled at the gringo. Now he was getting somewhere.

Walter paid for the gas with a bundle of small filthy bills and the attendant gave him one more appraising look. The gringo was covered in sweaty road grime—it was how he liked to travel in Mexico. He figured he did not look like an easy mark that way, or good pickings either—if he was dirty and stinky. Generally speaking, rich guys were clean and rich guys smelled sweet. Poor folk were dirty and poor folk stunk.

He pulled the truck over to the tacos while the child hitched a ride those hundred feet on his running board. Apparently, the chavo did not trust the gringo to actually pay off on his taco promise, he had probably seen too many promises go bad, and was going to keep tabs on him meanwhile, hold him to the tacos.

Walter ordered four tacos de adobada for himself and four tacos de lengua for the boy. *Para tomar*, he ordered a Squirt and a Coke. They sat on wooden benches and commenced to chow-down. The child dove into the tacos as though he was quite starved.

"¿Como te llamas?" Walter asked between bites. *How are you called?*

"Voy con usted, señor," the child replied. *I'll go with you, sir.* He spoke through a mouthful of tongue tacos and salsa picante.

"¿Como que vas conmigo?" said Walter incredulously. *What do you mean you go with me?* "Ni conosco de tu nombre." *I don't even know your name.*

"Gusano," said the boy. "Me llaman gusano." *They call me worm.*

WORM? thought Walter. Worm!

I'll show up back in Lake Tahoe with a truckload of dusty gliders and a grubby boy-child named Worm? How would that look? What will that do for my reputation?

"A lo major," he told the kid, "¿pero que es tu nombre, mijo? *Maybe so... but what is your NAME, child?*

Gusano took another bite of taco. He was very focused on his feast. "Dante," he finally spouted. Along with his name, a small brown projectile of food discharged from his lips, and landed somewhere on Walter's plate.

"¿Donde vas conmigo Dante?" the gringo inquired. *Where will you go with me Dante?*

"A su tierra," came the reply. *To your dirt. To your country.*

"Pero yo voy al sur," he lied again. *But I'm going south.* There was little point in subterfuge with a ten year old; Walter was just keeping up the lie.

"Lleva me con usted, señor." Dante reiterated, as though he either didn't believe the gringo, or didn't care. *Take me with you, sir.* After all—every gringo eventually heads north. Everyone knows that. They weren't called Norteños for nada...

"Ahhmm..." said Walter. "¿Y alli que hago contigo?" he asked. *And what will I do with you there?*

They all wanted something better of course, the downtrodden everywhere. Dante would want out of this truckstop taco stand, out of this dusty village, out of his own personal *infierno*. He probably didn't even know what was out *there*, he knew only what was *here*.

How would the child fare in Gringolandia? speculated Walter... He knew many illegal Mexicans in his home turf. Most of them were taken advantage of as cheap labor. Often they lived in abject poverty and squalor, a dozen of them in a single filthy room. In the summer, they worked long hours for little pay. When it snowed ten feet in the winter, they would be cold and hungry too, rather than just hungry. They would miss their families, they would work for next to nothing...

The grass was always greener though, on the otro lado...

"Chambiar," answered the worm through his tacos. *Work.* He took a long suck on his Coke and belched up through his runny nose. "Trabajo." *I'll work.*

"¿De que?" asked Walter. *At what?*

The child shrugged his shoulders hopefully. He pulled another dirty rag/wad from his pocket, and held it up as testament of his worth and ability. It must have been his back-up grubby ragwad because Walter had disposed of the original grubby ragwad in the trashcan at the pumps.

"Limpio vidrios," he declared. *I clean glass.*

There was no denying this child. No bringing him along either of course. Heck, Walter could barely take care of his own sorry self, let alone himself and a small illegal alien too. Resigned, they finished their food in silence, Walter listening to the heavy trucks roaring through town. Dante awaiting his destiny. Walter anxious to carry on the journey. Dante eager to get started on his own.

Culiacan was the next stop on the map—some three hours north. The gringo didn't like to drive at night, but he was prepared to do so now. There were the same innumerable hazards on the highway during daylight of course, but they were harder to spot at night. Cows and goats and dogs liked to sleep on the warm road. Unmarked curves and broken pavement lurked ahead. Suddenly, for no apparent reason at all, the lane would end; rocks painted white would appear in the headlamps and the driver would have to swerve to avoid disaster. For reasons Walter would never understand, eighteen-wheeler trucks would park in the road for the night, just park there like they belonged, the drivers could be seen sleeping in hammocks slung underneath. It was loco!

The intersections were poorly marked and it was easy to get lost at night.

And... there were the rumors...

Rumors of bandidos del camino.

Highwaymen.

Always the rumors.

"¿Usted viaje solo señor?

Are you traveling alone sir?

Walter would feel better after midnight. After midnight—there was virtually no other traffic. After midnight—when anything and everything on the road could be regarded as a life-threatening hazard or personal threat and treated as such.

∿∿∿∿∿∿∿∿∿∿∿∿∿＿＿∿∿∿∿∿∿∿∿∿∿∿

At least at night you knew the score.

Worm wiped his mouth on a grubby shirtsleeve and polished off his Coke with a very adult belch. Walter hadn't noticed 'till now, but the chavo's shirt was festooned with a faded image of Buzz Lightyear. TOY STORY it read across the front. The shirt was so gray with dirt that the words and image were barely visible, but it was a flying T-shirt in some silly way. In fact, Walter had silly old flying T-shirts himself—he collected them. One of the most threadbare he kept for cleaning his own windshield, stashed under the seat in the Ford, and it was in quite better shape than the Worm's. It was too small for the gringo, and it would be very big on Worm, but maybe he would grow into it...

He stood to make an exit. Dante stood too, and followed behind Walter to the Ford. Walter got in, slammed the door and fired up the engine. With a bit of tongue taco on his lip, Dante stood without moving as Walter threw him first the T-shirt from under the seat, and then as he fished around in the console for a tarnished ten-peso coin, and tossed him that too.

"¡Adios, Dante!" he saluted.

"¡Hasta luego, señor!" returned the worm. *See you later!*

"¡Hasta luego, Dante!" he agreed. Another lie, knew Walter; he'd never see the little worm on the highway of Life again. The child turned to walk off and he saw the back of Worm's Buzz Lightyear t-shirt. Buzz held his arm aloft and declared;

"To infinity... and beyond!"

The gringo chuckled at the absurdity of it all, and he looked carefully for speeding traffic as he pulled away thinking, *south, south, I'll leave town headed south for a bit and then I'll turn around to be sure I'm not followed. See how smart I am...?*

He was confused for a moment about which way actually was south; the twin gas stations were confusing him and of course, he had confused his own self with his anti-bandito ploy. In the darkness that had fallen during his roadside respite, it was hard to remember which way was which...

Finally getting his bearings, Walter drove to the edge of the village and pulled off the side of the road. Looking back, a road sign marked the village:

'La Esperanza'—*The Waiting*

Or The Hoping. It was all the same, he knew; in Español, 'waiting' and 'hoping' are the same word. What does that say about a culture? Anything?

He sat along the highway for a moment, waiting/hoping with his lights off, and rolled himself a fat joint. He reached into the bed and pulled an icy beer from the cooler. Ready now, for another three hours of intense driving, Walter turned the Ford-From-Hell around and aimed her to carry on. Soon he roared back past the PEMEX stations. It was a dolorous place at this hour. The traveler found it comforting that no cars or trucks were at the pumps—no banditos lurked in the shadows. As he sped past, Walter could see the attendant, slouched into a chair, waiting/hoping for something to happen. For the end of his shift...

Dante was still there, but when Walter gave him a shallow wave, the boy just stood there and watched him disappear down the empty highway.

Hoping.
Waiting.
La Esperanza.

~ᕙ≥≤ᕗ~

Walter and the Ford sped through the darkness for two hard hours. Left again with his own thoughts, but feeling contented now, the flier daydreamed about all the flying that lay in store on his homeward journey... about his arrival in Lake Tahoe... the bitchin' flying at Slide, Zulu and Daydreams... The sexy sluts at the North Tahoe nude beach who sunned themselves with their legs spread wide... Especially that horny bitch Kathy... Maybe this summer he get his hands on her... Friends and fliers from years gone by... All the partying they would do together... It would be great to get home to the High Sierra.

> *Home! Where my thoughts escaping*
> *Home! Where my musics playin'*
> *Home! Where my love life's waitin'*
> *Silently for me...*
> -Simon and Garfunkle

Gradually, the lights of a major metropolis sparkled on the distant horizon. Walter figured them for Culiacan. He was thinking how the time/distance had passed so quickly, that Culiacan should still be an hour and a half distant. Then he navigated another curve and the mistake became obvious and horrible as a battered roadsign swept past. It read...

TROPICO DE CANCER

Its message shown back on Walter, glaring in his headlamps, seared across his brain.
Tropico de Cancer!
TROPICO DE CANCER!
"FFFUUUUCCCCKKKK"
Tropico de Cancer!

~~~~~~

He slammed on the brakes and swung off the pavement and his dust overtook him in a tailwind. He spun the Ford back around to the sign and sat idling alongside the road. There it was—irrefutable proof that he had been traveling the wrong way these last two hours: The Tropic of Cancer!

"Fuck!"

The gringo wasn't such a wise traveler after all...

The gringo was a... *pendejo!*

He stepped out of the truck to stretch, and pissed on the same wet spot he'd created just a few hours ago.

¡Chinga les!

There was no point in lingering. Walter jumped back behind the seat, floored the throttle and headed back north with another curse. Four hours of his life was burned up in spent fuel and he was no closer to home. He was even getting hungry again...

~₪≥≤₪~

Two hours later, the lights at La Esperanza once again pulled into view. The gringo was tired and discouraged by then. He pulled into the same PEMEX station where he'd been four hours earlier and shut down the engine on the edge of the lot. All was quiet now. He stepped out in the darkness and emptied the beer from his bladder with relief and then, crawling in back of his truck, he quickly fell into a troubled sleep. In his dreams he was waiting and hoping and he was waiting and hoping... endlessly waiting and endlessly hoping. For what he knew not...

The waiting was quite hopeless.

Not a dream at all really, it was a *pesadilla!*

The next morning Walter's slumber was interrupted by the rumble of diesel engine as a trucker pulled in for fuel. He rolled over and just as he hoped to return to sleep he heard tiny knuckles rapping on the side of the truck. He opened one eye, enough to see the Worm peering back at him, hopefully.

"Buenos dias, señor," came the greeting. *Good morning sir.* The worm seemed happy to see the gringo.

Walter flopped back down in bed. He remembered Dante's final salutation last night. 'Hasta luego' he had said. *See you later.* Could it be that somehow, the child had known?

But Worm was plenty confused himself. First, the gringo said he was going south, only to leave the station heading *al norte*. Minutes later, the gringo had sped past and given him a little wave, now speeding *sur* as he said he would, blowing by like the wind. Now here, just at dawn the next day, here was the gringo again, apparently going *norte* now, much like a Norteño should if he had any sense. *These gringos sure behave strangely*, he concluded. *Maybe they really are loco, just like everybody says.*

He stood on tiptoes, the better to peer into the Ford. It was full of strange and wonderful stuff, and there were long colorful bags on a rack that spanned the entire vehicle from bumper to bumper.

Surely there would be room to hide up there, he hoped. Stow himself away for the journey.

Throat parched with morning thirst, Walter sat up and peered back through one exhausted eye at the chavo, who wore his new flying T-shirt, the one Walter had tossed him, the one that was way too big for him. It was just one of the many flying shirts Walter loved. This one declared:

"THIS IS YOUR BRAIN" on the chest and "THIS IS YOUR BRAIN ON A HANG GLIDER" on the rear.

Worm smiled at the gringo and, considering how early it was, he was bright-eyed, bushy-tailed and seemed quite happy to be there.

"Voy con usted, señor," said the Worm with hope renewed. Hopefully, his wait was over. He held up a grubby cotton wadrag as a sort of token of his worth. "*Trabajo,*" he said.

Laundry Day in Old Mexico or, Flight Of The Gringo

Walter pulled the Ford-From-Hell into the beach party in San Juan de Tenayác. It was Semana Santa—the Holy Week—and it seemed as though half of Mexico had come to this beach for vacation, worship and most of all, to party down. Driving slowly onto the sand he was sandwiched between an old horse-drawn wagon full of happy balloon vendors dressed in ragged clown suits, and an unidentifiable motor vehicle crowded with four cotton candy machines. As far as the eye could see the beach was covered with tents and awnings and cardboard shacks built to withstand exactly one week of heavy usage, then to be abandoned as just a memory, left to the sea and the tides, the only force on Earth powerful and sure enough to clean the beach after the Mexican Easter fiesta. What the Mexicans had in mind was to party down for seven days, while consuming all sorts of comestibles and inebriates, and then to leave everything behind right where it falls. But the huge piles of trash had yet to form—it was Party Time.

Walter drove slowly through the sand towards where a hang glider king post was sticking up, just visible above the crowd. This was camp for the Colima pilots, who were already well established on the beach and ready for the big fiesta. While pulling into the campsite, Walter noticed with relief an old señora in her shack across the way, as she was hanging out wash to dry on a line. He had a large bag of dirty clothes himself and was becoming a stinky gringo—a *gringo pestoso*. He made note that he would take them to her and strike a deal to have them laundered.

Jesus and Geraldo greeted him then, each with a bottle of vino in hand. "Valter, Valter, Bienvenidos!" they said. Welcome! They seemed genuinely happy to have the gringo show for some flying up and some partying down. Jesus already displayed a notable swagger and was typically muy macho. He was decked out in spandex shorts and flip-flop sandals and a muscle shirt Walter had given him which delivered an important message across the chest:

WILL FLY FOR SEX

"¡Hola, amigos!" said Walter as he slid from the truck. "¿Que tal la fiesta?" he asked. *How goes the party?*

"¡Esperando de ti!" said Jesus. *Waiting for you!* It didn't look like Jesus, or anyone else for that matter, was waiting for anyone at all. The bottle he swung at the end of two fingers was already half gone. It dangled cap-less around his knees and Walter figured that soon it would be just another piece of trash lying on the beach. Jesus took a serious swig from the bottle, some of which swilled down his chin. He wiped his face and offered the bottle to the gringo. "¡Vamos a volar!" he suggested. *Let's go flying!*

Jesus didn't look in any shape to fly, which means he was in his typical flying shape. Jesus was a ranchero who flew only on weekends. He drank only on weekends too, and was often quite inebriated by noon—a condition he commonly flew under. While Walter didn't approve of this type of behavior, there was nothing he could do to prevent it. And who was he, after all, to pass judgment of or mess with local custom?

Geraldo, on the other hand was quite different from his flying buddy. Geraldo was the absent-minded professor type. A real professor at the trade school in Colima, Geraldo would only sip at the bottle when it was offered. Walter got the impression that he didn't actually drink anything. He would only go through the motions, then grimace a little and make grunting noises. It was a means of retaining his machismo without actually having to suffer the inebriating consequences. Geraldo, too, was wearing a shirt with a message in English. It read:

I LOVE EVERY BONE IN YOUR BODY. ESPECIALLY MINE!

He sidled up to the Ford now and shook hands with the gringo. "Se entra el viento," he observed and pointed his finger at the nearby mountain peak. *Here comes the wind.*

"¿Donde esta el despegue?" the gringo asked. *Where is the launch?* Geraldo pointed to a distant overlook where a few cars were parked. Tourists were admiring the view and a statue of Cristo Rey that had been built there. "¿Alli es?" he inquired. *That's it?*

It was very small. Walter had been expecting something more lofty. This place looked to be about fifty feet above sea level, maybe a hundred. It didn't look very soarable, but immediately behind it was a very tall mountain ridge, a good two thousand feet tall. "¿Es todo?" he asked. *That's all?*

"¡Sí!" said Geraldo happily. "Quando chupa el viento, se puede surfear." *When the wind blows you can surf it.*

The wind will have to blow pretty damn hard thought Walter. There were a couple of frigate birds working the tiny lift band at launch as they watched. These are the most talented of soaring birds, somehow they could stay aloft effortlessly, even in calm air. But the ridge rose precipitously and dramatically behind the overlook; maybe there was potential there after all. If you could work the lift and climb a little, it looked very soarable up there indeed. When Walter's gaze just naturally turned skyward he noted the red-tail hawks, the buzzards, the frigates and gaviotas, and just about anything and everything else with feathers and a beak seemed to be circling around up there. Some were dotted out and circling in lift so high they could barely be seen. Walter wanted to be there too—it was a longing that ruled his soul.

"Quiero llevar mi ropa susio hasta la señora alli," he said, pointing. *I want to take my dirty laundry to that lady.* He pointed at the señora who was still hanging clothes to dry. He stepped out of the truck and Jesus poked the bottle at him.

"Aguardiente," he smiled. The distillate is an anise-flavored brew, very sweet and strong. Favored by the lower classes because it is cheap, aguardiente is like drinking fire, but with a pleasing licorice aftertaste. Walter pretended to take a swig from the bottle, much like Geraldo would, just to placate Jesus. To decline would be an insult. Jesus slapped him on the back in happiness. "¡Buen amigo!" he declared. *Good friend!*

The gringo fished around in his clothes bag and he dug out a fresh t-shirt—the last of his clean clothes—a shirt he had been saving for just this occasion because it too offered an important message:

I REMEMBER WHEN SEX WAS SAFE AND HANG GLIDING WAS DANGEROUS

While Walter gathered up his clothes, his amigo kept up a constant dialog about what had happened on the beach last night, how everyone had gotten drunk, there had been some fights, and some good wrestling with the local chicas in the bushes behind the dunes. There was a gringa down the beach that Walter must meet, he said.

Together, they walked across the sand to the small 'palapas' shack where the laundry was hanging out to dry. All during the Holy Week, this woman and her daughters would toil day and night washing clothes by hand. There were two yearly pilgrimages for Mexicans to the beach: Christmas and Easter. The women probably earned fifty percent of their total yearly income during those times, speculated Walter, washing clothes for the multitudes.

Walter and Jesus approached the old señora to strike a deal. The señora hefted the bag and did a mental calculation. She opened the throat of the bag and poked her nose in there, for a simple inspection or to judge their level of filth Walter could only guess... How much elbow-grease would they need?

"¿Trais jabom?" she asked. *Did you bring soap?* Walter had not—it was a variable the old señora would have to consider in her calculations. "Vente dos mil," she announced. *Twenty-two thousand pesos*: about seven dollars. Walter thought the price seemed a bit steep but quickly agreed anyway, he wasn't about to bargain with an old peasant lady for her living. Besides, he knew that his clothes would be boiled and scrubbed neatly folded and returned cleaner that they had been in months. Looking forward to the afternoon of flying, they quickly closed the deal. And then the fliers headed for launch.

~ᗰ≥≤ᗰ~

The flying had been surprisingly good from that tiny viewpoint bump. They took off at just fifty feet or so above the crashing surf below. But the wind was straight into launch and picking up as they stepped into it. The beach, crowded though it was, stretched away below the cliff and offered a measure of safety to the tiny launch. It was blowing straight into the ridge behind, so with a shallow right turn away from the threatening waves Walter and Jesus and Geraldo had managed to climb up the ridge and disappear over the hills for a marvelous afternoon of soaring with the birds. They worked their way far back from the beach, inland where there was nowhere to make an emergency landing should the wind stop suddenly, but the windsign on the water would warn them of that. After a couple of hours, Walter tired of the smooth ridge-lift and flew down to land on the crowded beach.

He bagged the glider and watched Jesus land, and then Geraldo. Soon the three fliers were basking in an assumed glory—los pajarombres, *the birdmen*, of Tenayác. It could be only a matter of time, they were sure, until the women came and offered themselves up to the brave heroes.

They commenced to party in earnest meanwhile, and Walter cracked a cervesa.

"¿Quando vas a hacer nos un chubi?" asked Jesus. *When will you make us a fat doobie?*

The gringo had scored some weed from the kids in Picila, the tiny town where they frequently landed their wings, and he remembered how foolish he'd felt buying pot from kids. He knew they would need some 'mota' at the fiesta though. Jesus hardly ever smoked pot—he preferred the aguardiente. But this was a PARTY.

Walter decided the time was right to roll one. He turned to the Ford to grab the bag when it hit him: he had stashed the pot in a pair of dirty shorts for the trip and hidden them in his dirty laundry bag! Then, he had spaced it when he gave the bag to the old señora to wash! The old señora and her daughters had the bag of pot!

Oh sweet Jeezuz!

In a panic Walter stopped everything. Even now the señora may be notifying the Ruráles, the Estatáles, or maybe even the dreaded Federáles. At this very moment, several branches of Mexico law enforcement must be descending upon the beach to scoop up the pothead gringo and throw his ass in some dim dungeon of despair. His head spun and his heart raced. Frantically, he began to gather up his loose stuff and toss it in the Ford-From-Hell. He would have to load his glider too.

Was there time?

What time was it?

Maybe he should just leave the glider here for Jesus? Abandon it, and run like hell? You can't fly in prison, that much anyway, was certain.

Desperado!

Jesus noticed the sudden change in demeanor in the gringo—the sudden flurry of hurry.

"¿Donde vas, amigo?" he asked. *Where are you going friend?*

"¡Norte!" said the gringo. "¡A mi tierra!" *To my country!*

"¿A tu tierra?" grinned Jesus. *To your country?*

These gringos were a very unpredictable bunch. One moment they were here to party and smoke a joint, and the next they were ready to drive two thousand miles home! He would never understand them.

"¿Por que vas alli?" he asked. *Why are you going there?*

"Mejor me voy alli que quedar me aqui en el carcel," explained Walter. *Better I go there than stay here in jail.*

Jesus gave him a funny look. "¿El carcel?" he asked with astonishment. "¿Como que el carcel?" *What do you mean jail?*

Walter jumped on the glider rack of the Ford-From-Hell. He was furiously tying down the stack of wings as he explained:

"Dejó la mota en mi ropa susio." *I have left the pot in my dirty clothes.*

Jesus continued to look astonished at the gringo. "¿Y?" he asked. *And?*

"¡Y quiero desapear antes que llegan la ley!" *And I want to disappear before the law arrives.*

"¿QUE?" said Jesus. His eyes bulged and he plunked the bottle on the hood of the Ford. *What?*

"Tu me escuchaste," said Walter. *You heard me.* "Tengo que ir..." *I must go...*

Jesus let out a loud burst of laughter. "¡La mota!" he hollered. *The pot!* "¡En tu ropa, con la abuela... las policias!" He was summing-up the situation in his mind. *Pot in your clothes, the granny... the police!* He sure seemed gleeful at this news, and was having a good laugh at Walter's expense. But his delight only made the gringo more paranoid—some of these people might overhear him and get suspicious.

"¡Dejame en paz, cabron! ¡Tengo prisa!" said Walter. *Leave me in peace you prick. I'm in a hurry!* At this Jesus let out a loud whoop and slapped his thigh in a Mexican expression of mirth. He didn't seem concerned about Walter's dilemma and predicament, at all.

"Calmate Walter," he said. *Calm down!* "La vieja no llame la policia." *The old lady won't call the police.* This news didn't convince Walter.

"¿Como sabes?" he asked. *How do you know?*

"Por que la vieja no le gusta las policias tampoco," said Jesus. *Because that old lady doesn't like the cops either.* This advise came as a bit of a revelation to Walter, but he continued to ready the Ford for some fast travel. Jesus continued: "Aqui en Mexico las polícias son como perros. Peor que peros." *Here in Mexico the police are like dogs.*

Worse than dogs. "Nadie les confian." *Nobody trusts them.*

This much was true, Walter knew. You never saw one or two Federáles or Estatáles or Ruráles. Cops, however you called them, seemed always to travel in groups of a half dozen or more, as though fearful that some bato might take a pot shot at them if they were ever caught alone. Jesus spat to emphasize his point.

"Chinga les!" he declared, then "Vamanos por la bolsita," he said. *Let's go get that little baggie.*

Walter and Jesus walked back across the beach to where the clothes were hung to dry in the breeze. The old señora still toiled at her chores— there would be little rest for the weary of Tenayac for these next few days. "Desculpe, Doña," began Jesus. *Excuse me, ma'am.* She turned and recognized the gringo.

"Oh," she said. "Dejaste algo." *You forgot something.* She reached into her apron and handed Walter his bag of pot. "Aqui," she said with indifference. *Here.*

Walter took the bag and tentatively looked around, feeling foolish and suspicious too. He jammed it in his pocket and thanked the señora, nervously.

"Gracias Doña."

Jesus grinned some more and slapped Walter on the back. "No te preocupas," he said. "Aqui andas con amigos." *Don't worry; you're among friends here.* He turned to the señora and said his gracias.

She grinned and her wrinkled face split like old parchment. "Esta feo la yerba," she said. *That's some really bad herb.* "Tengo mejor si ustedes quieren." *I have better if you want.* Walter couldn't believe his ears.

"¿Como?" he asked. *What?*

"Sí," said the señora. "Lo uso por mis ojos." *I use it for my eyes.*

"¿Por sus ojos?" he asked.

"Si, tengo glaucoma, pero veo bien por la yerba." *Yes, I have glaucoma, but I see fine with the herb.* She beckoned Walter and Jesus through the gate in her fence. Together they entered her dusty, dirt floor living room, Walter had to duck under the door to avoid banging his head. Then, beneath the 'palapas' roof as the surf crashed outside and the crowd partied down, the old señora twisted up a joint.

"Cuando quiero leer tomo un chubi," she said. *Whenever I want to read I smoke a joint.*

Walter felt great relief. He wasn't sure if a joint would help his reading, but he was willing to try. Meanwhile, he silently hoped that maybe some day, somewhere... it might help his writing.

Flight to the Ancient Island City of the Pendejos or,
Not Just Your Everyday, Garden-Variety, Dumbasses

pendejo noun, *pen-DAY-hoe*
1) A pubic hair
2) Mexico slang (pejorative) A stupid person; a dumbass
-- From Wictionary.org

"You're flying where?" asked my gringo friend.

"We're flying to the ancient island city of the pendejos," I replied with as much levity as I could summon. "More prosaically known as Mexcaltitán or Mexcaltitlán, depending on which map you read. Probably nobody knows for sure—they are, after all, pendejos."

My friend gave us a bewildered look. "What's a pendejo?" he asked.

"That depends on what diccionario you read," I said. "But In Mexico it is used to mean 'idiot' or 'fool'. Ancient island city of the Pendejos."

My student/co-pilot piped-up at this. "I thought 'idiot' is 'idiota'," he said.

"Goes to show what an idiot you are," I explained. This got me a punch in the shoulder from my student/co-pilot, who is a big gringo and who packs quite a punch. "Ouch!" I cried. "The diccionario I have clearly lists the literal meaning of pen-DAY-hoe as 'pubic hair'." This bit of wisdom got the chuckle I was hoping for, so I elaborated a little more. "Male," I said.

My amigo and my co-pilot looked at each other and then at me. "Male?" they asked in harmony.

"Sí señores," I said. "Not to be confused with pen-DAY-ha with an 'a'. Pendejo, pendeja."

"Pen-DAY-ha?" asked my gringos. "What's that?" Quite obviously, they were not linguists.

"Pendeja, with an 'a', is a female pubic hair of course." I was pleased to dispense with this rare tidbit if wisdom and get the rise from my amigos that I'd been hoping for, so I reiterated; "Today we fly to the ancient island city of the pendejos. I suppose there will be pendejas too, if you look closely. Saddle up!"

"Why in hell would you want to fly there?" I was asked. We were, after all, standing in a real-life Triker's Paradise, a fabulous place to fly, a beautiful bay called Bahia Matachen, or Mantachen, or Matanchen, or Mantanchen, depending on who you ask, or what mapa you use to find it. It would have been easy to just stay put right there and fly up and down the beach—an exercise I have never quite tired of, and great practice too.

"Good question," I replied pensively. "Because we love to fly? Because we crave adventure? Because I am a bit of a pendejo myself? Because I'm wild about pendejas? I'm not sure really, but from the few photos and postcards I've seen it looks like it will be a spectacular sight."

"But... City of the Pendejos?" they asked. Why don't you just call it Mex, Mexca... Whatever it is?"

"Kind of hard to say ain't it- mex-cal-ti-TAN or mex-cal-TIT-lan; not even the pendejos know for sure. Most gringos see that name and get their tongues all tied in knots when they try to say it. I know I did. Now try this;

"Ahh-TEE-goo-ah see-you-DAHD EEZ-lah day loz pen-DAY-hose."

My amigos gave it a good try, but came up short. "Sort of rolls off the tongue don't you think?" I asked. "Ancient Island City of the Pendejos."

"How far away is it?"

"Not sure of that either," I reply. "But El Totopo has flown up there and seems to think it is about an hour and ten minutes as the cuervo flies. That's in his wagon of course; mine is a bit slower."

"Who is El Totopo?"

"David Henly," I said, "Chip," pointing a finger at my gringo friend. He was even now making final preparations for our flight, fueling-up, polishing his helmet visors, checking his camera. "'Chip' for short," I continued. "'Totopo' is Mexican for 'chip'. You know—*guacamole con totopos*. El Totopo has actually laid eyes on the legendary place of the pubic hairs from above. Today, he will be our flying guide. Hey Chip!" I yelled. "If you get too far ahead of us in that speedy wagon of yours, you might have to wait up for us slowpokes. Maybe even circle a time or two, whatever it takes. Bueno?"

"Sí señor!" my guide agreed. Satisfied, I returned to my own preparations for flight.

My amigos' look of bewilderment had become one of concern. "Do you have enough fuel for that much flying?" he asked. "Get you there and back too?"

"Can't say for sure," I reply. "But now that you ask, I am starting to feel rather pendejo myself. I suppose then, that it is only natural that I should want to fly to the ancient city where all the pendejos started from in the first place."

My amigo just shook his head sadly and said nothing. My student guffawed and shrugged his shoulders.

"It's a good thing I've learned to trust you or maybe I'd just stay right here," he said.

"We're bringing an extra six gallons of fuel along though," I said as I pointed to a red plastic Walmart fuel jug that I had lashed to the trike. "See how thoughtful we are?"

"How you gonna put that fuel in your tank," my amigo wondered. "Can you do that while you're flying?"

"Don't be such a pendejo," I returned. "Of course I can't put that fuel in my tank while I'm flying. We will have to land somewhere convenient and pour it in."

My amigo grinned at us and shook his head. "Where will you land? Is there a strip or something?"

"Don't know that either," I said. "But El Totopo claims there's plenty of fields along the way. We'll just pick one that looks good and make a fuel stop." I nodded and tried to look wise. "It's all part of the adventure of flight; we're pilots you know." I said. Then I turned to my co-pilot, "You ready amigo?" I inquired. "Saddle up! Vamanos!"

~ᴎ≥≤ᴎ~

The pendejo who sprayed us all with gravel and beach sand one afternoon was really and truly a pendejo. He showed up at the campground on a busy Sunday afternoon in an SUV with windows tinted so dark we could not discern the occupants within, and no sooner did he hit the beach than he started doing donuts in the sand like a real pendejo. With wheel hard a'larboard and the throttle floor-boarded, he made several reckless circles. He was a pendejo, and he was a real menace too as he swung 'round and around until suddenly POW! there was a loud explosion due to having just popped both beads off the rims of both tires on the outside of the turn, such as I have never seen happen anywhere to any vehicle before.

Dead in the water now, all four doors opened suddenly and an even dozen people piled out. There were four adult couples in various stages of confusion or anger and four squalling children, also confused and angry. Music, so loud that it was distorted beyond belief or even comprehension, also poured forth in confusion.

The driver seemed very agitated by this turn of events, and was also clearly belligerent. Within moments however, he was set upon by the Policia Touristica, in their very first police-action that I have ever witnessed from them. Previous to this moment, the Tourist Police had done nothing more than drive past now and then and wave at us tourists. They seemed to be permanently on call. But now, with dispatch, they wrestled the belligerent pendejo to the ground and smashed his face into the sand where he was quickly out-gunned, out-manned and incapacitated.

Later, it must have taken quite a while just to get the sand out of his eyes, ears, nose, and throat.

A few minutes later I noticed yet another pendejo. This one had loaded four children in the trunk of a Volkswagen beetle—think about that for a moment now: *the trunk of a Volkswagon beetle*, and he went driving happily out along the beach with his head out his window so he could see where he was going. Sort of...

I have seen few drivers with such small regard for children in my days—he was just a typical pendejo.

Every day, pendejos arrive at the beach and drive out on the sand like they know what they're doing and they get stuck within moments. Then they proceed to dig themselves in deeper and deeper until they are hopelessly bottomed-out and yet; they sit there with their foot on the gas and continue to roar their engines, rocking to and fro, spinning their tires uselessly, digging in...

They remind us gringo tourists of small children with new toys that they haven't quite figured out yet. They are pendejos and there just ain't no better word!

Pen-DAY-hose

Of course, there are stupid people everywhere, and the author himself claims no immunity from idiocy—he has done stupid things himself. But generally, stupid people are not labeled as pubic hairs everywhere you go. Only in Mexico, at least as this traveler knows, is this term prevalent. You hear it every day.

"Es pendejo" and "Que pendejo" are words you hear everywhere. And guys—don't forget the feminine—pendeja!

"No seas pendeja!" *Don't be a pubic hair (female).*

"El habla puro pendejadas." *He talks pure pubic hairs (idiocies).*

In Mexico, the litterbug pendejos are too numerous to mention, but they leave their trash behind with no thought whatsoever and so that deserves mention.

I was walking the beach with Sarge and we came upon a mess left by some pendejo who had not just thoughtlessly littered the beach with discarded beer bottles, but he/she/it had deliberately broken those bottles, smashed them to bits, leaving the beach scattered with shards of broken glass. For a gringo whose mother slapped him at the first sign of littering, for a gringo whose worst admonishment as a child was to be called "litterbug", for a gringo who cannot so much as toss out a bottle cap without feelings of guilt and remorse, it is just disgusting.

"Pinche pendejo cabron!" *Cheap pubic hair asshole!*

Every morning the pendejos put their bags of trash out in the street for the dogs. Of course, the trash is not actually left for the dogs—it is left out for collection. But since there are no containers to keep the dogs out of the trash, and since the dogs in Mexico feed primarily on trash and are otherwise neglected, there is trash scattered everywhere, by the starving dogs, long before the trash man arrives.

Does this make sense to anyone?

Late one night, as we gringos all slept peacefully, lulled by the song of the surf, a pinche pendejo cabron pulled onto the beach in his motor vehicle and threw her into park right outside my door. Then he turned his Mexican polka music up full-blast, so loud that it was totally distorted and you could feel the bass woofer THUMP THUMP THUMP! He woke the whole damn place up at 3AM.

"Pinche pendejo cabron!"

When the sun rose the next morning and we looked out our door, there was a small pile of trash he had left behind.

I was driving along beautiful Matanchen Bay, or whatever you might call it, I was headed north from the Triker's Paradise to find a cell signal, and I had my Honda 90 wrapped-out at full throttle, which yields a heady velocity of eighty kilometers per hour. I was overtaking a slow-moving lead-sled, which was belching a foul cloud of particulates in its wake, as though it desperately needed a valve-job. Clearing the left lane for oncoming traffic I swung wide to pass this stinking vehicle, when suddenly a bag of lunch-trash was tossed carelessly, mindlessly and, I might add, hazardously, into my path. The trash bomb came from the rear driver's-side window and the pendeja who tossed it out did so with narry a glance behind for traffic. The trash hit my scooter right on her bow. The litter went flying and the ice from some beverage broke over my ankle painfully and startlingly.

"PENDEJOS!" I hollered as I sped past even though, technically, she was a pendeja; I saw her startled look as I overtook them and I flipped them the Bird, a rude gesture not commonly used in Mexico, but which should see more action.

The pendejos who ride their motorcycles, scooters and quads with their helmets on but the strap not fastened—and there are plenty of them— seem particularly pendejo to this writer. Do you suppose they think that in case of vehicular accident the helmet will thoughtfully fly through the air with them and accompany them to the crash scene, where it will actually do its job? What sort of pendejo would even bother with a helmet if they are not going to fasten the strap? They say, "Oh! There's a helmet law in Mexico... I must wear it."

Does the law not include some verbiage like ' must be securely fastened'?

Examples of pendejos abound in Mexico. Thusly do the Mexicans describe their idiots, their fools, their pubic hairs. It is a word that I have long been fascinated with, especially the female gender of course—pendeja—some of which I have even been truly enamored of.

~ฑ≥≤ฑ~

On a lark, we set sail out of the Triker's Paradise with a compass heading due north. We had only a vague notion of where we were going, or exactly what we would find once we got there, or even how we would re-fuel, but our little plane purred along nicely. Our objective was clear: get aerial photos of Mexcaltitlán or whatever it is called—the Ancient Island City of the Pubic Hairs.

To revisit Mexican history again, legend has it that some centuries ago, in about 1000AD if I recall, an indigenous tribe who reportedly lived on this island, had a shaman who insisted that they must depart their island homeland and go in search of their own private Idaho. According to the wise guy—who must have been a bit of a pendejo himself—his people would recognize when they had arrived at the Promised Land because they would find an eagle, sitting on a cactus, holding a serpent in his claws.

~~~~~~~~~~~~~~~~~~   ~~~~~~~~~~~~~~

Being, one can only speculate, a rather foolish bunch, these people—who called themselves 'Mexica'—spent some forty years wandering and searching and looking for their Promised Land. We gringos can only be grateful they did not head north for Idaho in any literal sense (they did that much later of course) but finally beheld their vision in the high mountain valley of Tenochtítlan. There they settled and built more island cities and pyramids and proceeded to rip the beating hearts from the chests of everyone they could get their hands on, who was not Mexica.

To the other indigenous American tribes, and even unto us gringos, they became known as the 'Azteca', but to them they were still the 'Mexica' and they must have been pendejos indeed—otherwise how could eighty-three stinking Spaniards with a few horses and dogs have conquered the whole sorry bunch?

Ultimately, the conquerors proved to be even more pendejo than the conquered and, after a few centuries of imperial cruelty, the Mexica would rise up to slay their conquerors, to reclaim their land, and to cast off the moniker the Españoles had given it of Nuevo España, which is why this land is known today as...

México...!

It is also why even today, the Mexican national symbol and the Mexican flag bear the eagle/cactus/serpent vision.

But it all started at the ancient island city of the pendejos and so we were going to fly there, like Quetzalcoatl himself—another ridiculous legend that ultimately came to pass.

"Clear prop!" I hollered to my student. Then, "Step on the gas! Now push the nose up! Now point her north! Hooooee!"

We took off in front of El Totopo with the idea of getting a head start but he soon overtook us and before long became just a tiny dot on the horizon. Then I blinked and he was gone, disappeared, vanished in the Wild Blue Yonder which, given his promise to wait up for us, makes him a bit of a pendejo in my book. I hope he can forgive me... We were on our own now. It was true enough though, what El Totopo had told us about landing fields— there was no shortage of them. Croplands stretched in all directions.

This was good news because a glance at our fuel level let me know that we were burning our tank at a rapid rate. Two big gringo pendejos trying to fly fast enough to catch El Totopo were burning two hours of fuel in about one hour. Happily, after about forty-five minutes, the ancient island city became apparent in the distance off our starboard bow, in the middle of huge estuary wetlands.

It exists!

If we hope to get photos of it though, we would need that extra fuel that was strapped to the plane. There did not look like anywhere to land on the island itself—I suppose the ancients had not thought of a runway for their village—and the fields ended a few miles before we would arrive, leaving nothing but marshy wetlands and sloughs.

"We better start looking for a place to land," I told my student. "Don't look now but we're about out of gas."

"No shit?" he said, and contorted himself around to get a good look at the fuel tank.

It is a transparent affair, transparent so the pilot can see its contents and check the level; there was no doubt about our fuel situation. Back at the helm now, he cast his gaze about below. "Plenty of fields here but doesn't look so good over there, humm?" He pointed at the Island of the Pendejos.

"We better pick one of these fields and hope for the best," I suggested. "Can you tell me where the wind is?"

There wasn't much doubt about that anyway; we had been bucking a headwind since leaving Matanchen. We both agreed that the wind was coming in off the Pacific and so picked us a field that looked good from above. It was a dried-up saltpan and we had a nice long run at it with plenty of room to set down and so we bailed on in for a smooth touchdown—straight into the wind. When we touched down we felt like a couple of pendejos though, or at least I did, because the field we chose was filled with dried-up cattle hoof prints and clods of dirt like rocks. It was really ugly.

What the chingada would I do now?

My student was happy so far though—we were on a big adventure—a lark. We quickly filled our fuel tank with our spare fuel, which would give us plenty of flight time to get the photos we coveted and get some lunch at a sleepy little beach village and ride the tailwind home too. The only problem was, "I sure don't like the looks of this runway for taking off."

"What do we do then?"

"I'm gonna see if I can't find somewhere better," I said. I walked off to the north and I wandered aimlessly about, in much the same manner as must have the ancient pendejos themselves while they were searching for their Promised Land. I walked and I walked and finally I found a place that looked much better for take-off. There was no eagle, no cactus and no serpent to let me know, but there was a semi-smooth runway oriented nicely into the wind. It was not as long as I'd have liked, and there were head-high bushes at the far end, and it still looked like a desperate make-it-or-else operation the likes of which I prefer to avoid, but what else could I do?

I was a pendejo.

Trying to make light of the situation, I stumbled back through the rough and faced my co-pilot.

"What do we do now?" he asked again.

"We drag it over there," I pointed. "I don't even want to taxi through this crap."

"Drag it huh?" came the reply. "You want me to push, or pull?"

We pushed and pulled and dragged the trike about a half-mile through the saltpan from Hell. An occasional cow pie reminded me of just how pendejo I can be. We stopped a time or two to quench our thirst with the water I had thoughtfully brought along, and about that I felt better. Finally, we settled on a smooth spot that offered a reasonable runway, and we walked it and cleared it of any incidental obstacles, sticks and clods of dirt or rocks and piles of cowshit.

"I think I better take the front seat if you don't mind," I said.

"Be my guest," came the answer, which was really a twist on the truth. After all—he was my guest.

We saddled up, fired her up, warmed her up and then pushed her nose all the way up. I stepped on the gas and aimed her straight into the wind. I was glad I had a slow wagon at that moment, because she jumped off the saltpan so quickly I heaved a sigh of relief. We weren't out of the jungle yet though, until we had climbed on that little two-stroke engine, myself just praying to the ancient ones, and to Quetzalcoatl too, that she would not quit suddenly, climbed to an attitude sufficient for an emergency landing back on the saltpan if we had to. By then we could clearly see the ancient island city of Mexcaltitlán, pretty as you please, sitting incongruously enough on a tiny spot of land in the middle of a muddy and pestilential estuary.

"No wonder them Mexica went a-wandering."

"That is bitchin'!"

"Pretty cool, huh? So it's not just legend after all..."

"And you say this is where the pendejos come from?"

"Originally, yes. Sí señor."

"Wow."

We circled and circled and exposed the roll of film in the camera that was hanging from the wing, dipping the trike this way and that for the best angle, at which point we leveled the wing and headed for the beach about five miles to the west.

We turned south when we were over the wide beach and we followed it along to the tiny pueblito of El Estero where we hoped to find our promised huevos rancheros. As we approached the little village we found El Totopo wandering the sky looking for us and suddenly, we weren't feeling so pendejo after all. Together now, we landed on the big wide beach and walked up to a ramada in good spirits. We all ordered huevos rancheros and we were all served huevos ala Mexicana instead. But of course—we were in the land of the Mexica after all.

~ฎ≥≤ฎ~

I stepped out of my motor home and there sat a pendejo in the driver's seat of his compact Chevy sedan. He was giving me a blank stare, like maybe a gringo was some sort of curiosity. His stare said,

"Duhhhh. Look at the gringo."

For reasons I didn't ask, he held a Kleenex to his nose. As I watched his every move, he gave a slight blow through his naríz and wiped at the resultant mocho. Even at a glance I could see he was a real pendejo, because of the pile of Kleenex—obviously his own, used Kleenex—on the ground under his left elbow, right where he had carelessly tossed them out the ventana. Suddenly indignant, I knew it was time I better leave Mexico; irrationally, I had come to hate Mexicans.

~~~~~~~~~~~~~~~~~~~~~~~~~~~~~~~~~~

"Desculpe señor," I said while pointing at the trashed Kleenex pile. I said 'señor' even though he was much younger than I. "Es de usted?" I asked. *Excuse me sir. Is that yours?*

His eyes flitted to where I was pointing and he just barely shook his head in the negative, as though I would believe such an obvious lie. Apparently, I was not dealing with just a simple run-of-the-mill, everyday pendejo, but with a liar too. A *pendejo mentiroso*. I decided I wasn't going to let him get away with such a lie so easily.

"La basura," I insisted and pointed again. "Es de usted?" I asked. *The trash, is it yours?*

This time he nodded an affirmative. It was a very slight nod, almost imperceptible, and it was accompanied with a vacant blink. It didn't take a genius to see what a pendejo I had at hand, but maybe he was not a mentiroso after all.

"La vas a dejar alli?" I asked. *Are you just going to leave it there?*

This time the pendejo wagged his finger at the gringo as if to say, "What do you think I am, a pendejo?" But the pendejo made no move to actually pick up his basura.

I knew my anger was at the edge of boiling over; here I was deep in Mexico, about a thousand miles south of Nogales, and suddenly I hated Mexicans.

All of 'em.

I jumped on my Honda scooter and blazed out of camp. I drove for five minutes and the wind in my hair cooled me off. I turned around and drove back to camp, to find that the pendejo mentiroso had departed, his pile of trash was all that was left of him.

Well, no... it wasn't quite all.

There was another pile of trash, just a few feet away, on what must have been the other side of his car. An empty Coke can, a tattered Fritos bag and a dirty diaper marked the former location of the pinche pendejo mentiroso's lovely wife and child. It had been an entire mini-family of pendejos.

I knew it was time for this gringo to pack up and head north. I leave this whole country to the pendejos and the mentirosos, let the trash be their lasting tradition.

Meanwhile, if I see an eagle, sitting on a cactus, with a serpent in its claw, I'm going to do my best to run that fucker down.

Treasure Of Sierra Grande or, Legend Of El Indio Alonzo

"¿**V**an a saltar ustedes señor?" he asked. "¿Ustedes van a saltar?"

It was a question that always astonished the gringo, whenever he was found on a precipice setting up a wing. So, under the circumstances, he just kept moving, ignoring the peasant. The peasant repeated himself, which as Walter saw it, was totally unnecessary.

"¿Van a saltar usted señor?" he asked again. "¿Van a saltar señor?"

On yet another beautiful day, the two gringos had spread colorful wings and were busy stuffing battens above a cliff on an isolated mountain in central Mexico, and there would be no respite from the scorching tropical sol except to fling themselves off the edge. That was the focus and that was the objective and that was the urgency: set up and get the chingada out of there. If they kept moving and kept hydrated they would probably be okay. If they stopped what they were doing and let that sun have at them they were certain to either slowly deflate or downright blow a valve.

But the peasant was, if nothing else, persistent. He turned to Dahveed and asked the same question, "¿Van a saltar ustedes?" He spread his arms to animate to situation, he pantomimed a buzzard in flight and his eyes took on a lofty focus. For a moment he was Quetzalcoatl, returned.

"Ustedes van a saltar?" he asked.

Of course the gringos were gonna saltar.

What a stupid question.

This is why they had driven for days to get here, bought the Mexican auto insurance, paid all those hefty tolls to the greedy cabrones in their little toll booths, braved the kids and drunks and cartels and the loco drivers and the legions of other obstacles and hazards from Nogales to Colima, just to arrive here under the sweltering Mexican sun, on the side of this particular precipice...

Were they gonna saltar?

Does El Papa wear a funny hat?

¿Why else had the gringos loaded up earlier in the day and driven up to the flanks of Sierra Grande, an imposing massif outside of Colima, Colima, Mexico? ¿Why would they be suffering so to get all set up...?

...to saltar...

Any pendejo could see that...

¿What did the peasant think—that they would make such plans and spend such money and take such pains... just to look good on a dusty mountain road on the side of a cliff in the middle of nowhere? ¿That they might set up their fancy wings and wait for someone else, maybe someone even braver or... or dumber, to take over? ¿Some other pendejo would saltar? ¿Perhaps they would just take a few photos and then put the wings back in the bags— let's not and say we did?

It was a question Walter had answered a thousand times at a hundred different launches and each time it seemed a bit more ridiculous. So he ignored the peasant and his stupid question. Or tried to.

But the peasant was difficult to ignore...

The piasano was wearing a magnificent old sombrero made mostly of straw as usual, but with a leather panel atop the crown that gave him a distinguished countenance, a dashing bit of style the gringo had never seen before. A tiny tassel dangling from the brim at the rear kept him in a sort of perpetual motion. He wore an elaborate western shirt with piping along the shoulders and down each arm, prancing ponies embroidered on each shoulder. The sleeves were fastened with stylish snaps and he wore a leather vest and bolo tie over top. His trousers were quite grubby but they had recently been neatly creased somehow. They were fashioned from some sort of herringbone fabric that Walter had not often seen in Mexico. He wore a sash belt, the loose ends of which dangled below his right knee. Ostrich skin boots completed his attire, and Walter decided he cut a rather dashing figure as he stood on the edge of the cliff making like the Feathered Serpent himself, holding out his arms and imagining what it must be like to saltar from such lofty heights. As he walked along the cliff edge Walter could see from the tooling on the back of his leather belt that his name was 'Epifanio', and that he was a 'CHARO'. Across the back of his leather vest was an embroidered lasso and a splendid caballo. The lasso spelled the caballo's name: HIDALGO, it read.

Compared to Walter, who saw himself now as just a dusty aging glidehead gringo, togged in old flying rags and sweating like an army mule, he was a rather refreshing sight. Maybe the peasant deserved some sort of answer.

Finally, the gringo piped up. "Sí señor," he started. Then he lied. "Vamos a buscar del tesoro." *Yes, sir, we're going to look for the treasure.* Sweat spilled off his forehead and stung his eyes.

~~~~~~~~~~~~~~ _____ ~~~~~~~~~~~~~~

This statement caused quite a reaction from the peasant. He swung around from the cliff and inquired with his arms thrown wide, "¿El tesoro?" he cried. "¿EL TESORO?"

¿The treasure? ¿THE TREASURE?

In its way, it was another stupid question, but at least it was one Walter had not answered over and over, countless times to countless pendejos. As everyone in these parts knew, there was only one treasure to be discovered atop Sierra Grande, or one alleged treasure anyway. As Walter understood it, technically the treasure still belonged to the railroad and the bank from whom it had been stolen long ago, and so there was really little point in finding it. The Mexicans would just take it away from you without so much as a *muchas gracias señor,* so what was the point? It was a nearly un-negotiable treasure anyway, in the manner of treasures everywhere, since it was so old and composed entirely of authentic minted Mexican gold coins—pesos—the likes of which you just don't see anymore.

You couldn't just show up down at the cervesaria to buy your refreshing beverages with a handful of stolen gold coins. You don't just take them down to the gasolinera and say, "Lleno por favor." You can't even cash them at the banco for that matter. You try that, and someone would demand to know how you came to have such a rare currency. The story would come out that you—the gringo—had found the treasure that el Indio Alonzo had stolen away some ninety years earlier, the tesoro he had refused to give back to its rightful owners; the railroad and the banko. The same treasure that he had stashed in some hidey-hole up on Sierra Grande before they lopped his head off to make an example of him, and put it on display in the Jardin.

You found that tesoro fair and square and now you'd like some beer and tamales, gracias. Finders keepers, losers weepers... ¿How much are these things worth anyway?

Known variously as the Tesoro del Indio Alonzo and the Tesoro del Sierra Grande, the treasure that el Indio Alonzo had made off with was around $1,800 pesos, at a time when pesos were far more precious than they are today. No one knows for sure how much the tesoro is worth hoy and that includes this campesino, this paisano, this charo Epifanio but hey! If you find it, it will be party time one way or another.

¿Maybe there is still a reward...?

Of course, some bandido would steal it from you like they did to Bogey and his booty in Treasure of the Sierra Madre, the dirty hijo de puta! Or it might draw gunfire as did the suitcase full of cashola in El Mariachi, by some lousy hijo la chingada!

Walter was all set up and Dahveed was all set up and still the gringos kept moving at a steady pace. In the forefront of their minds, in their frontal lobes, that part of their brains which separates action from inaction, there burned the notion that one of them was going to have to help the other launch, to help him 'saltar' as it were. It was just common glidehead courtesy. And that would leave the other of them to launch himself solo as best he could—a frightening idea in such a rowdy place.

Of course, whomever 'saltared' first would be the 'wind dummy'—he could only guess at the conditions of the sky out front. Whoever 'saltared' last at least had some idea if he was going on a journey high into the Heavens, or conversely down into the burning Hell of the fields below. He could guess that by what happened to the wind dummy.

Either way, it was not an entirely pretty situation. Happily, it was the uncertainty of it all that the gringos craved.

Dahveed was laying out his harness as though there was no doubt. Walter turned his back on his task and took the four steps that brought him to the cliff edge to check out the launch conditions.

Launch, on Sierra Grande, is a flat road-cut bench in the mountain that leads to a narrow steel ramp that juts out from the cliff and down at about a forty-degree slope. The cliff itself is quite vertical for several hundred feet below the ramp, steep enough that you could not climb up or down it without great trepidation, you might only fall off into the hard rocks and cactus below. Which foolishness would lead only to tragedy Walter supposed. It was better to not think of doing it wrong, he knew, concentrate only on doing it right. Calm thy nerves and thy brain activity and focus thyself completely on external stimuli—in this case the wind. Run hard and keep the wings level, the nose down.

He stood with his toes on the edge of the ramp and watched the bushes below as they rustled back-and-forth in the thermals. A gust slammed him in the face, a hot gust, like it had maybe issued from the Fires of Hades itself, a gust that sounded a bit like a distant bulldozer rumbling up the mountainside.

But were the thermals strong and consistent enough to loft a bold gringo high into the sky on a flight of fulfillment?

Or were the gaps between thermal cycles lengthy enough to flush a foolish flier into the fields below?

It wasn't far down there really—only about eight hundred feet said the locals. Walter and Dahveed had scoped-out those fields on foot and found them to be rough ground covered with innumerable obstacles—rocks and rabbit holes and furrows, broken bottles and such, scorpions... and thick with spiny cactus and thorny vegetation. They had both just shook their heads and glanced skyward, silently swearing never to land down here if at all possible.

Back atop the cliff Walter stood in the hot blast for a few moments and Epifanio the peasant exhorted him to action.

"Salte!" he cried. "Brincate!"

Brincate, thought the gringo. Take it to the *brink*.

Brink it... *jump!*

Do it!

Now!

It was always the same.

He looked to Dahveed who was taking a long swig of bottled agua. He dropped the bottle into his harness and wiped the dribble that had spilled down his chin. Both gringos knew what the other was thinking.

"Go for it dude," he said. "*¡Salte!*"

"You give me a wire?" Walter asked.

He pulled a windbreaker over his tee shirt. It was the only garment necessary at such a scorching flying site. He pulled his Camelback over his arms and clipped the strap shut in front of his chest. He stepped through his leg loops and pulled the harness on over his shoulders—always an uncomfortable chore—then he cinched up his back strap. He stepped over to the wing and clipped the D-ring into the hang loops, connecting himself for better or worse to a hundred-fifty square feet of tubing, wires and sailcloth. Dahveed moved around back of the glider to hoist the keel level for the hang check. Then Walter lay prone in his harness, checking his suspension.

"Looks good," said Dahveed. It was all that needed to be said, and it was all the effort that might be wasted under the circumstances.

"You gonna ask the peasant for help?" Walter inquired of his amigo. Dahveed gave Epifanio a sidelong glance of speculation. If he was a quick learner, if he paid attention to what the gringos were about to do, if he took Dahveed's wires and helped him—just so—and then quickly got the Hell out of the way, he might be a big help for Dahveed's impending launch.

If not, it could be Disaster.

"Dunno," muttered Dahveed.

"Let's pick her up," said Walter.

With the wings level both gringos picked up the wing—Walter mostly in control but Dahveed standing by for emergency assistance. They carried the wing to the ramp with Dahveed holding the nose wires and Epifanio hovering near by.

~~~~~~~~~~~~~~~   ~~~~~~~~~~~~~~

"¡El tesoro!" he cried a time or two by way of encouragement.

El Indio Alonso has seen better days...

His ancient señora had appeared from his rattletrap old Datsun pickup and hobbled over to watch the exciting proceedings. She was wearing a full-length lime chiffon dress with many layers of skirts underneath, and fancy ribbons sewn here and there. Her pewter-gray hair was tied in braids and wrapped in similar ribbons. In a nod to fashion and modern industrialization, she wore stylish wrap-around reflector sunglasses.

"Van a buscar el tesoro del Indio Alonzo," her hombre explained enthusiastically. *They're going to search for the treasure...*

The struggle at launch lasted only a few minutes. Walter picked the wing up a couple of times but had to set it back down as the cycles from Hell grabbed it and tugged it this-way-and-that. Finally, the wing felt balanced long enough to give him some confidence. Freedom... well, the Laws of Physics anyway... was only a few steps away. Suddenly...

"CLEAR!" he yelled, and Dahveed did a great job of getting so; he dived to the right and to the ground and Walter took those three desperate steps which transitioned him from a mere earthling to a glorious birdman, a quick metamorphosis that was a leap-of-faith-in-yourself. The wing stayed level, the nose cut into the cycle, and the gringo was off clean. "WahOOO!" he yelled with relief, and immediately began to climb. He looked below and under his harness and watched as Dahveed picked himself up from the abyss and dusted himself off. By the time Walter began his first circle, he gazed down to see that his amigo was already stepping into his own harness.

While Walter dug into the lift and commenced to climb up the side of Sierra Grande, Dahveed clipped in, did a standing-hang check, then began inching his wing towards the precipice. He would pick the wing up a few inches, then set it back down a foot or so closer to the edge. Up-shuffle-down, up-shuffle-down, up-shuffle... and so it went until the flier was standing on the launch ramp just two steps from his own transition—Heaven or Hell.

In strong turbulence now, Walter was totally gripped on the control bar as he circled aloft and watched below with apprehension. Then suddenly it was over—or had it just begun?—Daveed's wing sailed clear of launch, and the day was on!

Now the job was just to wrestle with the lift and ride it as high as possible. Walter watched below as Dahveed too began his climb. He watched the charo and his pretty old señora getting smaller and smaller where they stood on launch and craned their necks skyward. Soon, they were but tiny ants.

¿What were they thinking?

¿Did they think the gringos were flying some sort of magic carpet, immune to the physical laws of the universe?

¿That they might just hover over the bushes, rocks, crags and cactus and casually scan every crevice for gleaming gold?

¿Did they believe the gringos were on a magic carpet ride? Just give them a few hours, a day or two at most, and they would be golden gringos, rich beyond their wildest dreams?

¿Gringos dorados?

Well in fact, they weren't on any carpet ride at all, magic or otherwise.

They were hooked into a hundred and fifty square feet of sailcloth, aircraft tubing and stainless wire, seventy-pound wings that were bucking in the thermal updraft like wild horses; imagine Pegasus with a fire under his ass. Icarus without the wax. Mighty Mouse on marijuana!

Gripped on the bars, Dahveed and Walter circled close enough to Sierra Grande to take advantage of the ferocious lift as it roared up the mountainside, but hopefully not so close as to dash themselves into it. For the next ten minutes or so, there was no thought of the Treasure of the Sierra Grande—or El Indio Alonzo either—only of survival.

~~~~~~~~~~~~~~~~ _____ ~~~~~~~~~~~~~~~

Soon Walter cleared the windswept heights of the mountain, at which point Dahveed had caught up with him. Together, the two gringos milked the last bits of lift, which carried them high above the mountain. Stopping to circle here and there, the gringos could finally enjoy the ride, revel in their success, and marvel at the wild circumstances that had brought them high over a brooding mountain in tropical Mexico. The air was smoother here, having spent much of its angry energy climbing to such heights, and much cooler too. In the near distance to the east stood the Fire Volcano Colimótl, spewing an enormous cloud of steam and smoke. Looking the other way, far to the west glittered the Pacific Ocean, a graceful curving coastline defining Mexico.

After half an hour of sightseeing, the gringos pointed their noses away from the mountain, saying 'Adios!' to Sierra Grande and its hidden treasure. They flew out and landed alongside the highway.

~רﬞ≥≤רﬞ~

They had made two successful flights, culminating in two successful landings. It was all the treasure they really hoped to find. With a refreshing fizz, the gringos popped the cervesas they had stashed away in their harnesses. They made a toast to El Indio Alonzo. Perhaps if the bandito had just flown a little he would not have been such a mean *desperado*. He might even have kept his head.

They released tension on the wing, pulled battens and folded up the sails.

It was as Walter was pulling the cover bag over the wing that he heard a car door slam and turned to find Epifanio and his señora parked alongside the highway. The peasant walked around to her side of the car and helped his señora from within. They carefully picked their way across the field to where the gringos had almost broke down, and gave them a warm handshake.

"¡Bueno, bueno!" he exclaimed. "¿Como estubo?" *How was it?*

"Well," said Dahveed, "Typico de Sierra Grande—fuerte, turbulento, chingon!" *Strong, turbulent, bitchin!*

Epifanio grinned at the gringos and nodded his head to agree, gazing at the distant mountains as though now he had some idea what it was like to 'saltar' from such a place, and turn into a little spec in the sky.

Then suddenly he turned his eyes to the gringos with the hundred-thousand-peso question on his lips:

"¿Y el tesoro?" he asked. *And the treasure?*

Aladino or,
Lesson Of The Rose Girl

Late afternoon sun filtered into the jardin like a soft gift from the gods, reflecting rays from the old cathedral across the narrow cobblestone street and etching shadows along the plaza walk. The small square in old Guanajuato, Mexico was coming to life with the promise of another evening's respite from the hot tropical sun.

Students from the nearby University hurried or strolled past, some with girls on their arms, some in pursuit of more mundane matters. Workmen were winding down their day, while nuns in gray habits ran who-knows-what errands.

I sat alone on an ornate wrought iron bench enjoying the scene, observed over the edge of the

Mexico City English newspaper called simply enough 'The News'. All my gringo flyers had returned to 'Gringolandia' and at the moment I felt like I was the last one left in all of the 'republica'.

Always intrigued by the social tapestry of Mexico, I found my attention more and more drawn to the activity around me, and less and less to the day's news. I was astonished by the sheer number of things happening around me, how the constant inter-action of people in Mexico seems such a natural occurrence. Perhaps these are all neighbors, I speculate, accustomed to borrowing eggs or a cup of asucar from one another. Chisme across the fence.

An old man approaches wearing a clown smile painted on his face and selling cotton candy. He eyes the gringo briefly as a prospective client, but is distracted as a pack of ugly stray dogs scurry past. Dogs in Mexico always look like strays to me I think. This particular pack is focused on a single bitch in heat. In fact, one lucky stud has succeeded in his efforts to mate with her and is now doing what only dogs are allowed to do in public. They scurry between us briefly, oblivious to everything but their own snarls and growls.

The old clown scowls through his smile and delivers a foot to the ribs of the nearest mutt, who howls in surprise and scurries off. Old clown departs too, intent on selling his wares elsewhere.

The 'camote' cart is being pushed through the jardine. A small wood fire can be seen in the bottom of the cart and the smokestack belches acrid wood smoke. Two young boys coax this strange apparatus along- it is far too cumbersome for one alone. Every five minutes or so the oven builds a head of steam which makes a shrill whistle as it vents as if to advertise 'comotes'—sweet potatoes—get 'em while they're hot.

Over yonder, there arrives a man on bicycle who jumps off and lifts his bike on to its kick-stand and quickly turns the seat around backwards. As he pedals his now stationary bike the rear wheel serves to spin a grindstone. Presto; instant employment! He begins to ring a bell by way of advertising that he's open for business—sharpening kitchen knives.

Over the edge of my news I notice for the second or third time a pair of little street urchins who are apparently selling roses. Guanajuato is a lovely old place and perhaps there are lots of lovers here, creating a glorious market for roses. They seem to be interested in me, these kids, or maybe in my silly headgear. But they are spying on me, slowly closing the distance with many giggles and much animation—pushing each other and shoving.

Suddenly the rose-boy is standing directly in front of me, staring at the blue 'saphiro' that is glued to my turban. It is just a cheap piece of costume jewelry really, and my turban is a fake piece of headgear, but kids always find it fascinating. I was wearing my turban because I'd been flying that afternoon and had a bad case of helmet hair I wanted to hide. The child stood before me and remembered his true mission: he thrust his roses toward me and stated his sales pitch. "Muy buen precio senor," he offered. *Very good price sir*.

If the child was selling nearly any other item I'd have probably bought with no hesitation, but what use did I have for flowers? They would only stink up my humble digs and remind me I had no one there to share them with. No novia, and no señorita, no amante and no señora to call my own—no girl to give the roses to. "Gracias compañero," I reply, "pero no tengo novia." *Thanks pal, but I have no girlfriend.* I shrugged my shoulders and hid behind the News. Not so easily deterred, the child just grins and thrust his roses at me once again, as though I should purchase them all.

Hummmm...

"I tell you what I'll do," I told him in my simple Spanish: "If you can just find me a novia I'll purchase all your flowers and then I'll give them to her!" I say this in what I perceive as a brilliant maneuver. What do I have to lose? "Until then I shall save my pesos for her arrival. So, run along now. There must be someone more interested than I. Someone who's already found his señorita."

Spinning on his heel the 'muchacho' runs back across the square towards his female counterpart, who is darling cute, but much too young for me— say, oh, about nine or ten years old—and who is already clutching an armful of roses of her own.

I return my attention back to 'The News', something about the 'Niners having kicked butt in the playoffs, but it seems like news from a distant planet.

I guesstimate that some two hundred pigeons are settling in to roost for the night on the facade of the old cathedral in front of the square. They whirl and spin about the evening sky, flying in tight and chaotic formation. The ancient church is a myriad of ornate carvings of saints and angels and the like, all of which make splendid perches for the birds who squat there on a nightly basis. The church is famous for this evening ritual and many flash bulbs are spent recording the nesting frenzy. The church is streaked with hundreds of piles of bird guano, some stacked so thick as to completely bury the occasional unfortunate saintly figurine in bird shit.

Tall slender senoritas stroll the courtyard but avoid eye contact with the gringo. They certainly are plentiful here, and they divert my attention. I am convinced that if I could but get my hands on one such angel I would find eternal happiness.

I actually smell the niña behind me before I see her. The same odor as her brother—roses and unwashed child—has approached me from behind. Imagine my surprise and delight to turn and see the rose girl now, as her accomplice pushes her the last few steps towards me. Then more boldly, as though she began selling roses at birth, the child is standing before me and holding her flowers.

"Desculpe señor," she says. *Excuse me sir.* The child's eyes are fixated on my gold turban. I could hardly wait to hear what comes next. Could this be the novia I'd requested from the rose boy? If so he had certainly acted promptly on my behalf. I would have to wait some years to reap my reward however; on closer inspection the child was even younger—maybe seven or eight I judge. Chocolate ice cream appears to have spilled down the front of a grubby flowered summer dress, she stood in scuffed patent-leather shoes, and she was missing two front teeth. Unselfconsciously she wiped her runny nose on a sleeve. Grubby fingers clutched her bunch of roses to her chest—a nearly overwhelming fragrance filled the warm evening air.

"Di me chiquita," says I, the lonely gringo with the cheap turban, "¿Como te ayuda?" *How can I help you little one?*

~~~~~~~~~~~~~~~~ ~~~~~~~~~~~~

The chica continued standing before me, apparently entranced by my headgear; she did not even press her sales pitch. But now she dropped her eyelids and hugged her flowers back and forth in her face. Finally she spoke.

"¿Es verdad que usted hace deseos?" she inquired. *Is it true you grant wishes?*

Suddenly I understood. Due to my cheap gold turban, these little callejeros had assumed that I must be Aladino, the famous genie himself, or someone with equally magic powers. Of course! Children everywhere know of Aladino and his Magic Lamparo. And, children everywhere have hopes and dreams—wishes. The child standing before me could use some new shoes. Hers were falling off her feet and the shoelaces had gone missing. Would she wish for a gift so sensible? Probably not, I decide. Probably, she will wish for some candy or a doll or... or a Nintendo for all I knew. I wanted to dismiss the child and tell her to just leave me alone, but under several layers of grime, she was darling cute. So I said to her:

"Sí niña, normalmente tres deseos, pero hoy falta solo uno. ¿Que quieres mija?" *Yes child, normally three wishes, but today there remains only one. What do you wish daughter?*

The rose girl stood briefly, happily, on her tiptoes and then rocked back on her heels. She gazed over my head towards the ancient cathedral for a moment and then leveled her eyes at mine. Finally she opened her mouth; "Que mi mama me quiere mucho!" she wished. *That my mother loves me a lot!*

Frankly, I was shocked. I wanted to grab this child and squeeze her full of love for being so sincere. Who knows of the relationship between this fragrant little rose girl and her mother? I certainly did not. Where was her mother anyway? Who supplied her with these roses and who collected the proceeds? Did she even have a mother? And what about the child labor laws here in Mexico? Did anyone care?

Those and a thousand other questions flooded my brain.

Still the child stood expectantly in front of me and awaited my grace. What could I do? Better she'd asked me for that doll after all, or the piece of candy or—some wish I could readily grant. With a wave of my hand and an 'Abracadabra!' I declared as best I could: "¡Sus deseos son ordenes!" *Your wish is my command!*

The child jumped with glee and ran wildly back to the rose boy, who had been watching the proceedings from a respectful distance. They embraced through bunches of roses, spun each other 'round and beamed of joy. Holding arms they disappeared running and skipping gleefully across the jardin.

I sat alone on the old bench in the old square in old Guanajuato for some time longer, uneager to spend another night alone. That was getting old.

I finally stood and strode deliberately across the square towards my humble hotel. Tomorrow was another day and there would be flying to lift my spirits. Always flying.

As I reached the steps to my room I heard a shrill cry from across the way:

"¡Señor!"

I turned and saw one last time, the rose girl and her toothy smile, as she waved me a tiny farewell.

Flight From Mexico or,
Death On The Highway

The three gringos had all hucked themselves off Cerro Potosi, an imposing peak on the road to Gringolandia. Their idea was to try to fly as far north as possible. North after all, was the way out— the way out of Mexico and back to Gringolandia. The winter flying season was winding down, the gringos were headed home, this flight was to be their last in Mexico Querido, the last of a long exciting season. Mañana, they would head for the border.

A thunderstorm was brewing to the south of launch as they set up their wings and laid out their gear, but the sky looked very promising overhead— light winds and perfect puffball cumulous clouds.

Sgary was first off and had a disappointing ride to the valley floor. He quickly bagged his wing, tied it down atop the Ford-From-Hell, and stood ready to race north after his two amigos. Walter and Larry hucked themselves off the mountain, and climbed immediately above the huge peak. They blazed on ahead of the storm, flying north in very buoyant air. Each time Walter slowed to climb in a thermal he tried to judge the storm as he circled.

Was it moving?

Was it moving fast?

Which way was it moving?

Was it expanding?

Would it overtake the gringos?

Would they have to run from the storm like frightened dogs with their tails between their legs?

Or...

~~~~~~~~~~~~~~~~~~~~~~~~_____~~~~~~~~~~~~~~~~~~~~~

Would it peeter-out and leave them soaring to blissful happiness and fulfillment, far away in some distant field of alfalfa?

Only Zeus the Sky God knew for sure.

"Que sera, sera," said the Mexicans. *Whatever will be will be.*

Meanwhile, there was lift abundant out in front of the storm. From his chilly loft Walter could see the curtain of virga hanging from the nearest edge of the storm and plunging towards the ground. The virga was rain of course; sheets of rain that did not hit the ground. Powerful thermal updrafts were preventing that.

But perhaps cold air was hitting the ground somewhere. This would displace the warm air and push it up in huge areas, and it was likely that even now the gringos were enjoying that benefit—there seemed to be smooth, fat lift everywhere.

Walter keyed the microphone on his radio, "How 'bout it Larry," he squawked over the air. "What about the storm?"

No reassuring answer returned across the sky however. If Walter squinted and concentrated, he could still see Larry, just a tiny dot out ahead of him, higher and further along the wind as he always seemed to be. Walter had no realistic hope of actually catching up with his amigo, and he accepted that reality. Larry was just too talented a flyer for Walter to keep up with.

In the words of Wingnut, another gringo glidehead and a mutual friend; "There just ain't enough mustard in all the World to cover that hotdog."

Well, you'd think he'd answer the radio, thought Walter, wondering if something was wrong with his own equipment. He turned the volume dial this way and that, turned the squelch off and heard reassuring static; nothing apparently wrong with the radio on his end. But he was not really surprised if Larry's radio was on the fritz. For all his talent in the sky, Larry always had the worst gear.

At fourteen thousand feet the thermal topped-out, so Walter quit circling and headed north once again. He held the bar level and tucked in his arms. He pointed his toes in his harness boot and tried to maintain best-glide airspeed. He flew like this for almost a half hour, covering maybe thirty miles. Meanwhile he never saw his amigo Larry again and, once out front of the storm, he never found any more lift either. Soon, he had glided all the way to a landing alongside the highway. He was relieved when his feet touched back on Mother Earth—the spent thunderstorm was still forbidding on the horizon.

Soon Sgary arrived with the Ford-From-Hell and together they made quick work of bagging Walter's wing. They tied it atop the truck and sped north, chasing after Larry.

"Looked like you guys were getting hammered by that front," recalled Sgary.

"Looked it I'm sure," replied Walter. "But it was quite smooth. Just big lift everywhere."

"Damn! I missed it! I love flying when it's like that!"

"I never found anything else though. I just glided to the ground. It was final-glide almost from overtop the peak."

"You gave 'er yer best..."

"Leave it to Larry to disappear in the sky."

"He's a dog."

~~~~~~~~~~~~~~~~ ~~~~~~~~~~~~~~~~

"He's an animal."

"He's half-bird you know..."

"He's all birdman."

"He's a goner all right."

"He's a hot dog."

The gringos drove in silence as the stereo squalled a rock 'n roll tune;

> In a place you only dream of
> Where your soul is always free
> Silver stages, golden curtains
> Filled my head, plain as can be

Larry was the best flier in Tahoe. He was one of the best athletes too, and his efforts and escapades were legend in the Tahoe area. He had come down to Mexico for some winter flying and had blown everyone out of the sky. The Mexicans didn't know what to think of Larry, because he often dressed caveman-style, a leather loincloth, suede moccasins, and a deerskin across his chest. A leather thong held back his hair, which looked as though it had never been cut. Larry himself however, seemed to be cut from stone. Furthermore, he was always game to jump atop a horse, any horse he encountered, and make the animal do his bidding.

Clearly, the Mexicans saw Larry as a loco gringo. They loved him.

> Now if I let you see this place
> Where stories all ring true
> Will you let me past your face
> To see what's really you

Finally, around a bend in the highway, Sgary spotted Larry in a field off the road. He had landed in a small field along the highway where they would have to pass right by. Soon they had picked up a happy, as usual, Larry, and were rolling north once again, sucking on cold cervesas. They were looking at about nine hours of driving to the border in Tejas.

But trouble lay in store for the glideheads, as it often will south-of-the-border. It was as though Mexico would not let them through quite so easily; it would exact a toll. Because, around yet another blind mountain curve, the three amigos slammed on the brakes and swerved for a mule that was struggling in the middle of the pavement. The beast had apparently been hit by some other vehicle just moments ago, and was trying to stand on what looked like two broken legs. It was a very ugly scene that Walter wanted only to drive around and forget. But Larry would not let him.

"STOP THE TRUCK!" he yelled. "LEMME OUT!"

There wasn't much Walter could do to argue, Larry had already popped his door open and was about to jump from the speeding truck when Walter applied the brakes. In a flash Larry was running full-tilt, sprinting back the way they had come.

After a moment of indecision Walter swung the truck about too, making a three-point turn of it, swerving recklessly around oncoming traffic. He stepped on the gas and gawked as Larry arrived at the terrified beast.

In a rodeo-like maneuver Larry jumped on the animal and grabbed the critter by the head, trying to break its neck. But the animal was just too big, too strong, and too panicked to be killed so easily—

it fought the gringo. It squealed like a horse, and it tried to bite its adversary. What looked like a broken rib protruded from the terrified animal's side, while blood and gore gushed everywhere.

Larry jumped clear of the beast just as the truck arrived; now he was covered in the animal's gore.

"We gotta DO something!" he hollered in the window. He was a wildman gringo gone loco.

"We gotta LEAVE!" demanded Walter.

"We can't just leave him here!" cried Larry. "We gotta put him away! Out of his misery!"

Walter begged to argue with the "we" part, but he knew it was no good—Larry was a cowboy at heart, he loved horses, and a mule was close enough.

The beast lifted his hindquarters and struggled to his front knees with terror written all over him, as a large coconut truck swung past the scene, its horn blaring. The mule's forelegs stuck out at horrible angles and left bloody swaths across the road with every movement. Again, Larry shouted;

"WE GOTTA DO SOMETHING!"

> Green grass and high tides forever
> Castles of stone souls and glory
> Lost faces say we adore you
> As kings and queens bow and play for you

Walter considered stepping on the throttle and just running the thrashing beast over—it seemed like the most efficient way to finish him off. But he was a very intimidating critter, and he flailed about wildly, teeth bared to bite someone. Instead, Walter shoved the tranny into park, scampered into the back of the Ford-From-Hell and lifted open the tool bin. In a flash he found what he needed and grabbed the hatchet. He stood up and hollered at Larry.

"Catch!" he yelled.

Nimbly, Larry grabbed the hatchet out of the air. It was a dull instrument, but it was the best Walter had to offer. He grabbed a tire iron from the tools and jumped out of the truck, to lend his own hand. But Larry was already at work, chopping horribly at the doomed animal's head as the beast thrashed about wildly. It took a dozen solid whacks from Larry, blood and guts flying everywhere, but finally the mule settled down and lay still, euthanized as it were, slaughtered perhaps, in a terrible bloody manner on the side of a Mexican highway, in the middle of the Sierra Madre.

> *Those who don't believe me*
> *Find your souls and set them free*
> *Those who do, believe and love*
> *As time will be your key*

By this time, Larry was covered in blood, slobber and gore. He was still panting with effort and excitement. He held the hatchet over the beast's head for a few moments and waved it menacingly. Then looked up to his amigos. Walter spoke:

"We gotta get the chingada out of here," he hollered. "No good can come of this."

But first, they had to get the carcass off the highway. Without discussion, all three gringos grabbed the dying beast by the rear legs and tail and dragged him off to the shoulder of the road. It was about all they could do to move him twenty feet. A semi-truck with a string of cars behind it sailed along the road headed southbound without hardly slowing, horn blaring at the gringos. Some of the cars honked too, and they all got a good look at the gruesome scene, the loco gringos with the dead animal.

It was time to hit the wind.

"Fuck! We gotta get out of here," declared Walter again.

The three gringos sprinted to the Ford-From-Hell and dove in. Walter spun the wheel and tromped on the gas. The gringos were still alive, even if they looked a desperate bunch.

It was just another crazy Mexican interlude.

"Fuck!" cried Larry. "Poor critter!"

> *Time and time again I've thanked them*
> *For a piece of mind*
> *They helped me find myself amongst*
> *The music and the rhyme*
> -all verse by The Outlaws

Gift Of The Pavo or,
To Every Turkey There Is A Reason

Walter's sore knuckle bled through the grease. Each time he moved that finger, the discomfort reminded him of his recent frustrations.

It had all started when he brought the Ford-From-Hell into the shop for a brake and bearing inspection on Christmas Eve morning. Taller Hermanos Santos they called the place: *The Saint Brothers Auto Repair*. On the sign above the greasy double-door entrance was an artist's rendition of the brothers themselves—Bomfilio and Napoleón. They stood in caricature with a wrench in hand and they smiled down upon the gringo. Over their individual heads each wore a sparkling halo. Somehow, Walter was not convinced of their sainthood, but they seemed to be reasonable wrenches.

The Saint brothers had inspected the Ford's running gear and recommended that Walter change the brake pads. They even offered to order the parts. Walter explained that he had a full group of gringo flyers for the Christmas holidays, that he needed the truck to go flying, and that he would like to schedule the appointment to have the pads replaced just after the Christmas holidays.

So the Hermanos Santos ordered Mauricio, who did all their real work, to mount the wheels back on the Ford while Walter went off to run some errands. When he arrived back at the shop, the Ford was parked on the bustling street. He had quickly paid Napoleon some pesos and driven home to load gliders and pilots. The clouds were already forming

~~~~~~~~~~~~~~~~~~~ ~~~~~~~~~~~~~~~~~~~

and the day was bright with promise for more excellent soaring.

The Ford had rocked 'n rolled up to launch full of good vibes and pilots from around the world and everyone had skyed out as usual. But as the Ford-From-Hell rolled down from launch something went wrong and Walter's radio crackled to life, his driver 'Chocho' on the other end.

"¿Valter, Valter habla Chocho. Me escuches?" he said. *Walter, do you hear?* The Mexicans, many of them anyway, could not say W—it came out as V.

"Sí Chocho, te escucho," repiled Walter. *Yes, I hear you.*

"La camionetta se descompuso," said Chocho. *The truck has broken.* They were the words Walter hated to hear. Perhaps there was some mistake.

"¿Como que se descompuso?" he asked. *What do you mean it broke?*

"La rueda se quito," replied Chocho. *The wheel has come off.*

The wheel? thought Walter. The wheel fell off? How could the wheel fall off? But of course, the Saint Brothers had just been at work on them. He scanned the road from his position overhead, following the dirt trail down from launch until he located the Ford parked near a field full of wild flowers and clover, a tiny dot far below, pulled half off the road and half on. Luckily, there was little or no traffic there to cause concern. He banked the glider slightly and drifted along high above the truck.

The other pilots in the air had undoubtedly heard the conversation, but most would not have understood the Spanish. "Looks like I've got vehicle problems, amigos," he spoke into the mic. "I'll have to go down and help Chocho. You guys better fly home to Valle."

There was some chatter about how Walter should just leave the truck where it died and groove on the awesome soaring conditions—deal with it later.

But by then Walter couldn't even hear the radio. Velcroed to the base tube as it was, and then stuffed to his waist, the velocity of the dive was enough to blow away the words. Walter banked into a wingover and let out the bar. As the glider slowed over the top a few words crept through: "...id you see that red-tail hawk...?" they asked, and then were blown away again as Walter dove for the ground.

Several wingovers and a spiral dive brought the gringo to a pattern altitude. Turning final Walter lined up over a field of milpa and headed towards the Ford. He could see he was lined up on the wind and so just let the glider float. Reaching the edge of the field he flared to a stop. He let his momentum carry the last few feet and set the glider down. He could see from there that something was indeed wrong; the wheel hadn't exactly fallen off, but the tire stuck out from the wheel well at a strange angle. He was glad that Chocho had enough sense to stop where he was. He stripped off his harness and went to investigate.

He found that the lug nuts were all loose. The wheel had wobbled badly and was about to fall off but had not. Two of the studs had broken off completely and the once-round holes in the wheel were now ovals. It looked as though the Ford needed a new wheel, which he had back in his hotel room, and a new set of studs, which he had not.

~~~~~~~~~~~~~~~~ ~~~~~~~~~~~~~~~~

He and Chocho managed to jack up the wheel and remove the lug nuts on the remaining six studs. Then they put the lugs back on with washers from the tool bin to take up the space of the ruined threads; it was a field repair with which they were able to limp slowly into Valle de Bravo and load gliders at the end of the day. It was nearly five PM and it was Christmas Eve when he arrived back at the scene of the crime. The Taller Hermanos Santos would be closing for three days, but Walter needed his truck. He didn't care if the Saint brothers had to drive to Mexico City and back for parts—he wanted his truck fixed NOW.

So he had been in a foul mood there in the taller—an angry gringo. The hermanos had agreed that they may indeed have caused the trouble by not tightening the lug nuts properly. Walter felt stupid for not inspecting them himself, but he played on indignity and anger and left the Ford there in a huff. If the Saint Brothers were going to live up to their billing, they would need a miracle to fix the truck for mañana.

As he was walking home his aggravation just grew. Here it was Christmas Eve and he was pissed off and needed to scramble for tomorrow's transportation. It looked as though he would have to rent a truck, desperate and expensive though it was. He had somehow to get his pilots on launch until the wheel crisis was passed. How would he do that?

He was walking through the crowded streets of Valle, all the shops decorated for Christmas and church bells ringing. Occasionally, fireworks exploded above the cathedral. He decided to take a longer route home and stop by the new gourmet

European grocery store that had become so popular with Valle's idle rich. Maybe a tasty purchase would chase away his foul mood. He had his eye on a smoked turkey for dinner. Maybe even a bottle of Courvoisier cognac.

He entered the store and noticed first off that Doña Teresa, who ran the boarding house where he booked his pilots, was at the counter inspecting the delicious meats and cheeses, the nuts and chocolates, the fresh-frozen jumbo shrimp and smoked Norwegian salmon. As Walter approached to offer her a greeting, he heard her ask the grocer, who stood across the glass display case something, but he couldn't hear what.

With the commotion of the other shoppers, and the racket from the street just three meters away, Walter could not hear the grocer's reply either. Instead he heard Doña Teresa ask again: "¿Quanto?" *How much?*

A cane truck rumbled by outside and the whole store shook as it passed, belching diesel smoke on the shoppers. Again, Walter failed to hear the grocer's reply. He saw only the look of disappointment on Doña Teresa's face as she turned away from the counter. She was peering into the small purse she carried and was counting some coins and she nearly bumped into Walter as she turned.

"Desculpe...Señor...Valter..." she muttered with a half-smile. *Excuse me Mr. Walter...* She seemed startled to see him there. She looked out of place too, among the other shoppers who were, for the most part, the rich Mexico City crowd. She looked as though she was about to bolt for the door, but Walter was in her way.

"Doña Tede," said Walter and nodded. It was a more respectful way to say 'Señora', but a more familiar way to say 'Teresa'. "Feliz fiestas," he continued, though he didn't really feel it. *Happy holidays.*

"Sí...." said Doña Tede. "Feliz fiestas." With another glance at the gringo she dropped her gaze to the floor, hurried out of the shop and disappeared into the crowd. As he watched her depart, he realized what a strong and good-looking woman she was—nicely shaped and with great legs. She had obviously been an attractive young woman, especially judging by her three daughters, each lovelier than the next. Walter suspected that she had been dealt a tough hand in life. He never saw a señor at her boarding house and didn't inquire why, but he had heard through the grapevine that Doña Tede was a single woman raising those three daughters and a son whom Walter had never met. That could not be an easy task anywhere, let alone here in Mexico.

Suddenly he felt very grateful for the life he led. Just drive around from one beautiful spot to another and hang glide. Fly whenever you feel like it and eat and drink your fill in between. Life's tough, or so they say.

"¿Le ayuda señor?" he heard. *May I help you sir?* Walter stepped forward now for his turn with the grocer. The man was very portly, as though having sampled all the imported delicacies of the world. Walter decided he wore a toupee and a fake smile too—a smile that showed impatience.

The gringo spotted a large turkey he wanted in the glass display cooler, surrounded by plastic fruits and vegetables in a gaudy fake cornucopia. A small sticker dangling on the turkey that read P36,000—about twelve dollars.

"Este pavo, señor. Quiero este pavo," he said. *I'll take this turkey.*

"Muy bien señor," said the grocer with approval. As he wrapped the bird he continued: "Estaba umado en Suissa. Muy sabroso." *It was smoked in Switzerland. Very tasty.* He handed the bundle to the gringo. "¿Algo mas?" *Anything else?*

"No gracias," said Walter, and paid the man. Then he paused. "Ahhh... sí señor. Una pregunta." *Yes sir. A question.*

"Diga me, señor." *Tell me, sir.*

"La señora que estaba aqui," he began. *The lady who was here...* "¿Que quiso?" *What did she want?*

The grocer looked askance at Walter and asked, "¿La señora que salio?" *The woman who just left?*

"Sí," nodded Walter. He held his hand up at about head level to Doña Teresa, who was quite tiny. "Doña Teresa," he said.

The grocer pointed at Walter's bundle and said with a nod, "El pavo, Señor. Quiso su pavo. Son muy popular." *The turkey sir. She wanted your turkey. They're very popular.* He replaced the fake smile and turned to the next customer.

Walter left the shop and stood on the curb in the crowded streets amid the rumble of holiday traffic. He felt sick. There he stood clutching the turkey Doña Tede wanted, probably for her Christmas feast. Walter remembered seeing the few coins she was counting in her purse. Obviously, there was not enough to cover twelve dollars pesos for a smoked pavo. What would she and her family eat for Christmas if not the smoked turkey?

Tortillas and frijoles?

~~~~~~~~~~~~~~~~~ _____ ~~~~~~~~~~~~~~~~~

He cared not to dwell on it, but the turkey felt heavy tucked under his arm. There sure was lots of food there—a feast!

Confused, he walked off toward home.

Rounding a corner Walter heard a sound that was strange to his ears here in Mexico. If he was not mistaken, someone, somewhere, was playing a violin. He walked on and the song became sweeter and clearer until Walter could recognize the tune as well. Ahead stood an old man playing The Little Drummer Boy on the violin. The sound was incredibly pleasing, although altered somewhat from the song Walter knew. But that was it unmistakably: Little Drummer Boy.

Walter stood by the old señor and listened for some time and was struck by the incongruity of it all. First, Walter had never heard a violin solo in Mexico. The only violins he had heard at all in Mexico were in the mariachi bands that stroll the streets and cafes. And also, to hear the music of a tune right out of his childhood... here on the street in Valle de Bravo... played by an old man... It was nearly too much.

It was Christmas Eve and he missed his family back in the states. He missed Tanya, who had left him for some other gringo who treated her better, or so she said. He missed Tanya most of all. He thought they had been very happy together just last Christmas.

Last Christmas....

Suddenly Walter knew what he had to do. He thanked the old man and dropped a few pesos in his hat. He spun on his heel and walked quickly up the street, now heading away from home. With luck he could catch up with Doña Tede as she walked to her humble casa. He hurried down the cobbled streets of Valle and dodged the cars, trucks, pedestrians, dogs and taco stands that clog the street. Suddenly the people appeared very festive to Walter, as if he just hadn't noticed before. He felt like he had been let in suddenly, on a special secret. Walking up the steep street to Doña Tede's casa the Turkey felt light now in his grip. He came to the large boulder in the street that marked her staircase and peered down the steep entryway. There was no one in sight, but Walter bounded down the forty-seven steps to her front door. The air along the way was sweet with the smell of her rose garden. A tiny but ferocious puppy, startled by the sudden appearance of such a large intruder, growled and barked at him.

Doña Tede's door was open, as it usually is. Walter had seen her shooing the chickens out of her house on more than one occasion. Standing in the doorway like some vision of loveliness was daughter number three—the youngest of the bunch, wearing a look almost as startled as the puppy's. Shockingly beautiful, in a budding sort of way, and painfully shy, she too seemed surprised, maybe even alarmed, at Walter's sudden appearance.

"Linda!" blurted the gringo. *Pretty!* Linda was her name of course, but in Spanish *linda* also means "pretty" or "beautiful". It was the first time he had ever called her by name. He thrust out his bundle of smoked turkey and Pretty took a step backwards. "Un regalo para ustedes," he blurted. *A gift for you!*

Pretty looked at Walter with surprise and wonder, maybe a little alarm on her face yet. Rather than accept the gift she closed the door slightly and hollered into the tiny house. "Mami!" she cried. The word floated out from her young and delicate lips and sounded like a sweet song to Walter, yet another Holiday melody.

"¡Mamiii...!" she sang again.

Doña Tede came to the door and found Walter standing there with arms outstretched. She stepped past her child and stood on the front step, now eye-to-eye with the gringo. She reached for the gift and smiled at Walter.

"Espero que ustedes gustan pavo umado," he said. *I hope you like smoked turkey.*

Doña Tede's eyes lit up, she smiled at Walter, revealing white, even teeth. Walter realized he had never seen her smile like that before. He felt, stupidly, as though he might cry and that wouldn't do at all. What would this tiny woman and her beautiful daughter think if they suddenly had a giant gringo all choked-up on their doorstep, sobbing on Christmas Eve?

"¡Feliz navidad!" he stammered.

With that he spun quickly and sprinted past the puppy, through the rose garden, and up the forty-seven steps he had just descended. Panting now, he turned his back on the staircase and strode rapidly down the street toward home. He felt strangely heavier without his burden. Then a shrill call came down the street behind him.

Music...?

A song...?

He turned and found Linda overtaking him from behind. She wore a light cotton dress and cotton stockings with a little ribbon in her hair. She was not so shy now, but she sure was Pretty. She stopped close to Walter and smiled at him. She stood on tiptoes and smiled some more. There was a flower in her hair and as the gringo watched she stuck her chest out at him. There were budding breasts under the lacy bra just barely evident through her dress. Walter was even more confused now, was he really lusting after this woman-child.

"Le invitamos para la cena mañana," she said. *We invite you for dinner tomorrow.*

"¿Quien?" he asked, dumbly. *Who?* He didn't know if he meant who, me? or who, you? or who, your mama? "Who?" was all he said. ¿Quien?

"Nosotros!" said Linda. *Us!*

"Me encantaria," he replied breathlessly. *I'd love to.* What he really meant was along the lines of: *My good God child, would that we could step into a chapel somewhere this very night and I could make you my child-bride. I would pledge to love and cherish you and you would teach me the joys of a simple life. I would stay with you and with your mama and I would never leave Mexico again. We will eat pavo and we will cross-pollinate!* But of course he didn't.

"¿Cuando?" he asked instead. *When?*

"Cuando tu quieres," she replied. *Whenever you like.*

"Despues de volar," he said. *After flying.*

Linda's eyes brightened at that notion. "Algun dia voy a volar contigo," she declared. *Someday I will fly with you.*

Here was news that stunned the gringo, and filled him with gladness.

"¿Cuando?" he asked again. It was as though young little Linda held the key to his happiness, but she had reduced him to monosyllables. *When?*

"El dia que tu me dices," she answered. *The day that you tell me.*

The conversation was getting dangerous now. What other delights would Linda offer up, standing here on the street as the sun set on Valle de Bravo on Christmas Eve, for only the saying?

"¿Hasta mañana, entonces?" said the gringo, finally finding his tongue. *Until tomorrow then?*

"¡Hasta mañana!" she agreed. She grabbed the gringo by the arm and pulled him to her and delivered a tiny kiss to the air about one inch from his ear canal, brushing her cheek with his meanwhile. It was the standard Mexican salutation, the same thing she might do with her brother, but it left Walter breathless and weak in the knees.

"¡Feliz Navidad!" she whispered.

She ran from him then, with a glance back over her shoulder. She tossed her hair back and forth as she ran up the street, she seemed light as an angel on the wing—as she was. She waved once from the top of the staircase and then disappeared to where she had come.

Walter felt like he was walking on air now—flying in a strange and delightful way. The anger and frustration he had felt earlier had vanished under these recent events.

He would have to hurry back to the Saint Brothers' shop right away, he hoped he wasn't too late. He would tell them to relax about the truck parts, to forget about it until after the Holy Day. To go home to their families. There were other flyers and other trucks that would go to launch tomorrow, he would find a way somehow. Let them go home, let them rejoice. He spun lightly on his heel and hurried down the street.

~~~~~~~~~~~~~~_____~~~~~~~~~~~~

Trikers Go To Morocco or,
A Stranger In A Strange Land

"We wanted something thoroughly and uncompromisingly foreign, foreign from top to bottom, foreign from center to circumference, foreign inside  *and outside and all around. Nothing anywhere about it to dilute its foreignness. Nothing to remind us of any other people or any other land under the sun. And lo! In Tangiers we have found it!*
-Mark Twain
 The Innocents Abroad

The Moroccan High Atlas

~~~~~~~~~~~~~   ~~~~~~~~~~~~~

On Friday, March 13, 1996 Walt Strzalkowski, his wife Rosilis and I boarded an Air France 747 for a flight to Paris. There, we were met by Thierry Caroni, owner and operator of the French adventure travel outfit called Veloce 21. We dined with Thierry at the Louvre, and then were escorted to another flight, this one bound for Casablanca, Morocco, where a fleet of European trikes and three-axis microlights awaited our arrival. During the following week we would fly a thousand-kilometer circuit of the High Atlas Mountains, culminating in the ancient city of Marrakech. The following is my journal.

Day 1 Casablanca to Beni Mellal– by auto

We are processed quickly at customs and ushered out to a waiting fleet of Mitsubishi PAJERO cat-cat diesels. "Cat-cat", it seems, is French for 4X4 vehicles. Our driver is a gringo who has lived in France for much of his life, Will Clarke, who is also the team doctor and emergency medical specialist. Will speaks English with an Okie twang, Spanish like a South American, and French like a Parisian.

We drive across flat, and then ever more rolling grasslands, which are surprisingly lush. Finally, a line of mountains becomes obvious through the haze ahead of us. The closer we get, the more imposing they look, until it becomes clear that they are a very steep and high range spouting from the flats- the Middle Atlas.

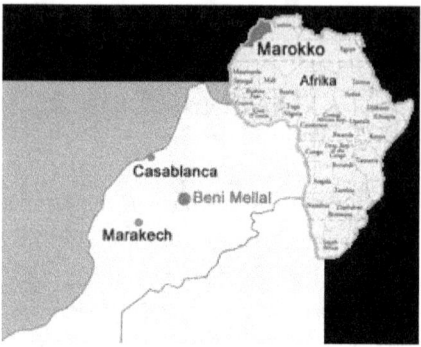

We pull into Beni Mellal around 3PM in the afternoon and get a quick bite to eat. We purchase some Moroccan currency, called dirham, and head out to the landing field. Following the GPS we get lost for a few minutes and have to backtrack. Finally, we find the field and inspect our aircraft. The Euros are busy setting up the planes and more or less disregard us. We find two Air Creation Clippers, three Cosmos trikes, two Albatross and one Minet.

We are at first told that there is but one trike available for six co-pilots, which is not at all how Caroni described things to us back in Paris and turns out, luckily, not to be the case at all. But neither is Caroni's version of the truth: we are five co-pilots for two trikes, which will mean that one of us is the odd-man-out. That would be me, I realize, since I am along as a guest, not a paying customer. This will be the third rally of Caroni's that I have attended.

The first—in Tunisia in November of '96—I knew that as ground crew, I wouldn't fly much. The second—In the desert southwest of the USA—I was a paid employee and knew I wouldn't fly much either.

This then, was supposed to be my turn.

The plan was for the aircraft owner to offer his spare seat to a co-pilot for each of the two daily legs. As the fifth co-pilot, there will be no opportunity for me to fly any legs. I am pissed, but what can I do? Make the most of it, I guess. I console myself that I will experience more of the culture of Morocco than the pilots who will fly over it all. Is this good? Time, and my journal, will tell.

Hotel The SANDS

At dusk it is off to our hotel, a humble place called Hotel Chems. I don't know what Chems means in Arabia, and I don't ask, but this place would more appropriately be called something like Hotel Eau de Gato: as it is crawling with felines, and there seems to be a perpetual cat fight going on out back, at what I can only speculate, must be the garbage heap. There are cats in the lobby, cats in the bar, cats in the dining room, cats in the halls. My room reeks of cats, cat piss and cat shit. Soon, my nose is running, my eyeballs are itching, my throat is scratchy, and I begin to sneeze. I can't decide what smells worse, the hotel room or our French pilot Pierre, who is indeed a ripe Frenchman. I will be glad to see the last of Hotel Chems, I am very allergic to the residents.

Leg 1 Beni Mellal to Er Rachidia

I am getting tired of driving on Caroni's far-flung adventures. Today I drive some more, and there seems to be no end in sight. Walt flew today, which is good because Walt paid good money to come on this trip. But he flew in the back seat, which is not what he had in mind, and not what he paid for. The idea at the onset was that Walt would sit up front in the pilot's seat, and do the pushing and the shoving. It must have been spectacular however, and it must have been cold, as he and Pierre flew over the distant snowy ridge and over ten thousand foot peaks.

Meanwhile, I drive with Dr. Will. We have an interesting interlude in a village called Midelt. Driving through this town, hungry, I spot some chickens roasting on a sort of rotisserie, Mexican style it seems to me. So I tell Sawbones we need a pit stop and he swings the cat-cat off the track and into a parking space. As we get out of the truck we are grabbed by the respective vendors of these roasting chickens, who charge out of their shacks, each fighting angrily over our business, until I think they will come to blows.

One of these men is armed with a tattered and weary old guidebook of Morocco, written in French, which is very torn, dog-eared and grease stained. Some of the pages are missing as though, perhaps, they have been used for very personal ablutions. But apparently, the author of this publication once made an appearance at this very chicken shack, and thought it notable enough to mention in his tome. Whatever; our host is waving his copy in our faces and hustling us to a waiting table. He first has his hand on my arm, then on my shoulder, then he puts his arm AROUND my shoulder. He smells bad. When I jerk myself away from him, the doctor scolds me, "You must treat these people with respect!" he commands. To the enormous disdain of the snubbed neighbor, I follow Dr.Will's lead and sit down with Mr. Guidebook.

Before long, we are served roast chicken and some other humble fare, and we are being hit on by a number of fossil salesmen.

That's right—fossils, it seems, are big business in Midelt. These guys are persistent from the start, and become downright rude as our lunch proceeds. They bring several fossilized snails and trilobites to our table, marvelous specimens, as well as some curious minerals and crystals, and insist we purchase them all, even though I have no interest in any. I am able to converse with them somewhat in Spanish, though our versions of the language are very divergent. I keep repeating "¡No lo quiero, no lo quiero!" which is such basic Spanish that anyone should understand. But it does no good. They keep repeating, "Buy eet! Buy eet! Very beeeuutifool!"

This scene continues as our food is brought, and our host, the noted chicken vendor himself, seems oblivious to our plight. A big grin on his face, he happily brings forth dish after dish of unidentifiable consumables, which we attempt to eat. I order a blended fresh orange and banana drink, which I find to be quite delicious and refreshing. But on the second drink from the glass, I watch startled as a fly, just one of the legions that call this place home, navigates its way into the beverage, and gets stuck in the frothy head. As it struggles to fly away, it only sinks deeper into the froth.

My host notices that I am distressed by the tiny critter. He snatches the glass out of my hand and, with a quick flick of his greasy finger, removes the fly. Then he hands me back the glass with a smile. His face shows great pride and satisfaction. He slaps me on the back as though to indicate what a good American I am, what a good sport. I swallow my pride and, trying not to think the worst about where that fly has been, and that finger too, quickly finish the drink before any other unwanted visitors dive in to spoil it completely.

Meanwhile, the fossil salesmen are becoming more frenzied and hard to ignore. One of them, whose name sounds something like Dweezel, invades my personal space. He actually sticks his face between my own face and the roasted chicken I am trying to consume, causing me pause. Had I been even marginally richer than I am, instead of trying to accomplish this journey on a shoestring, I would purchase the cursed fossils, just to be rid of this man. But when he smiles at me with black teeth, when the combination of foul breath and body odor becomes too overwhelming, suddenly I have had enough. I grab some of the stones that are on display on the table and backhand toss them, carelessly scattering them about the street. Dweezel looks dismayed and astonished for just a moment. Then he fishes into an old burlap sack where he keeps his supply of treasures, and simply produces more.

"Beeeuutifool!" he says. "Buy zzem!"

Moroccan treasure hunt

But it is as the doc and I make ready to depart the Midelt chicken rotisserie that things get dicey. Crossing the street to our vehicle, we trail a crowd of odiferous Moroccans; fossil salesmen, chicken salesmen, dogs, children, beggars and cripples. Only the chicken salesman is happy. While Doctor Will seems entirely unconcerned and strolls through the traffic like a prophet amongst his flock, I quickly lock myself in the cat-cat with the window rolled up and try to ignore the crowd. But Will lingers long enough with the door open, that some of them get their hands in the door. Then he rolls down the window and begins cursing at them. But with respect, I suppose.

"Dou dirham?! Dou dirham!" he shouts, which translates into something like, "Twenty cents! Twenty cents!" He is suddenly irate about something, and lets them know. I gather that they are trying to extort us for a twenty-cent parking fee.

I want to shout something like, "Hey dumbass! Pop the clutch, dumbshit! Let's get the Hell out of this disgusting place! Throw them twenty cents if you must!" But I don't. I figure: I must coexist with Will for the next week. I see no point in pissing him off on day number two. And anyway, he eases out of the crowd and we continue on our way.

"Do you believe that?" he asks, an astonished look on his face. "DO YOU BELIEVE THAT?!"

"Do I believe what?" I ask, not believing any of it.

"They wanted two dirham for guarding the truck!" says the Doc. "Sheesh!"

I suppose the most ridiculous part of this scene, is that the truck was just across the street in plain view the whole time, where a guard was quite unnecessary: who would they guard against? But I refrain from comment, just happy to be outward bound. I keep glancing behind us to see if we are being followed, as I am expecting Ali Baba and the Forty Thieves, but we are not.

We travel through some spectacular high country that is above timberline. Although we are very near the snowline, the rivers are dry, as though the parched earth has absorbed every drop of runoff. There is nothing growing more substantial than a few blades of grass, except in certain spots where they grow quite lush and add a pleasant green to the countryside.

Topping the summit and heading down the other side there is actually water in the river. There are nice turquoise pools and rapids and what looks like a trout stream. I don't see any fishermen, though. In fact, there are few people anywhere, even in the occasional collection of shacks and mud huts, most of which are surrounded by fortifications, as though they contain some sort of riches.

For one stretch of maybe a hundred kilometers I see nothing along side the road at all except for a few dogs. Dogs in the middle of nowhere, for no apparent reason, dogs who all seem to be starving, and I wonder why. I ask Dr Will, imagining he's versed in such matters. "Sheepdogs" he says. But there are no sheep, and he refuses to elaborate.

Finally we arrive at Er Rachidia, and we go to the airport where about half the fleet of ULs have arrived. Soon Walt and his pilot—our pilot—Pierre, appear from the northern sky, land, and roll up to the apron. I hang around until Pierre offers me the front seat of his Clipper and takes me out for a check ride. I give him three patterns with low passes and then grease a landing.

"Zees iz enuff!" exclaims Pierre. Apparently, I have succeeded. When we get out of the trike he proclaims, "Guud pilote!" Then Walt takes the front seat for his check ride. When they return Walt makes the mistake of asking, "So... am I a good pilot?"

Pierre points at me and says, "Bezt pilote!" I'm kind of embarrassed, since Walt has been flying longer than I, and has flown lots of different hardware; he is a more complete pilot and very capable with a trike. But I guess I should be happy. It's the Frenchman's trike, after all. If anyone is going to cut me loose with a trike, it is Pierre.

~ןɔ≥≤ןɔ~

"I picked up a book at random. Master, it is not written!"
"What do you mean? I can see that it is written. What do you read?"
"I am not reading. There are not letters of the alphabet, and it is not Greek. They look like worms, snails, fly dung...."
"Ah, well then, it is Arabic!"
- Umberto Eco, The Name of the Rose

نَ كُلُّ شَيْءٍ، وَبِغَيْرِهِ لَمْ يَتَكَوَّنْ أَيُّ شَيْءٍ مِمَّا تَكَوَّنَ.

فِيهِ كَانَتِ الْحَيَاةُ. وَالْحَيَاةُ هَذِهِ كَانَتِ نُورَ النَّاسِ.

If we travel much farther south into the desert, this road upon which we travel will peter-out in the sands of the Algerian Sahara at a place called Mhamid. If our current location is any indication of what Mhamid must be like, then Mhamid is indeed the end of the world as I know it. Most of the road signs about are in Arabic script that does indeed look like worms, snails and fly dung, but there is one sign here that catches my attention. It reads:

~~~~~~~~~~~~~~~~~~~~_____~~~~~~~~~~~~~~

I would rather spend my winter in the Bastille

In other words, if you get on your camel here and head south, you might make Timbuktu in 52 days. If all goes well that is... Frankly, if someone were to give me a camel right about now, I would turn the beast around and aim for Paris, and the sooner the better.

Our driver has announced that we are awaiting lunch, an event about which I fail to get excited. The idea of more of the same humble fare does not excite my palate, though my stomach growls. Oh well, I can stand to shed some pounds.

Leg 2 Er Rachidia to Tazzarine

When we arrive at Tazzarine, Dr Will is not sure how to get to the runway. We are navigating by satellite fix with the GPS, so we know the exact location down to, oh, plus or minus thirty feet. But we lack a map that shows which of the many tracks in the desert actually continue to the airstrip. So we drive a rocky dirt road until we are less than a kilometer from the GPS waypoint, where the road ends abruptly. Somewhere over the next rise is the airport.

Doctor Will decides to disregard the melon-sized rocks that litter our path and just forge ahead. He locks the gearbox in four-wheel low, and we lurch violently onward. When I suggest that since there is an airfield there must be a road somewhere and maybe we should just retreat and look for it, the good doctor looks at me as though I am quite mad, or have just sprouted a new nostril.

"There is no road," he states.

It seems then, that whoever is responsible for this road we travel and the alleged runway we seek, must simply have neglected to link the two. So Doctor Will flogs the throttle and we crawl painfully over the rocks, which scrape and bang the underside of the Mitsubishi in a disturbing manner, until we pull up on the runway. Later, another Frenchman who has been here before, one who knows the proper route, drives up the backside of the strip on a track, easy as pie.

My boredom is uninterrupted, until I am offered a quick spin in the Clipper around dusk.

Residents of Tazzarine

This is after spending nearly all day in the cat-cat chasing the trikes.

Pierre is, of course, my pilot. He does not hesitate to put me in the driver's seat again, although I can tell during the flight that he is nervous with my flying. I often glimpse his hands hovering on the rear wires.

After we pull away from the staging area I ease into the throttle, about half way. I do this for two reasons: a) I wish to spend as little time as possible on this dirt strip, sucking stones into the big red four-blade ArPlast prop at full throttle and, b) there are other trikers behind me who would be blasted by my prop wash.

But Pierre reaches through the seats and gives me full throttle anyway, about which I am surprised. And so are the trikers behind me, to say the least. I hear Doctor Will through the radio headset as he curses me for being rude. The other trikers are pissed at me, too, even though I was trying to be considerate. It was Pierre who was rude.

So I get my fifteen minutes of flying today, but I am less than thrilled. In fact, I am again impressed by what a slug is this Air Creation Clipper. Maybe it's the way that Pierre has the wing tuned, but it is even heavier in roll, if possible, than the other XPs I've flown. Also, it seems very slow to climb.

Oh sure, it is pretty... All painted up like a French whore. And, like a French whore, I may like to look at it. I may even like to ride it. But would I want to own it?

Tonight at dinner we are approached with the news that we must pay our fuel bills. This is the second time we have heard this theme, and it is becoming a drag. When Walt and his wife agreed to join this expedition, it was under the agreement that the price was all included, that there were no hidden expenses. Now it seems as though this was a lie. In fact, on top of the $2,600 they have paid in advance, there is a fuel bill, payable tonight.

Since Caroni has not accompanied us on this sojurn, and is probably still eating snails and drinking bubbly in gay Pareé, we cannot dispute these charges with him personally, and must take up the issue with his staff, none of whom speak English except the doctor, who wants nothing to do with this debate. When Walt produces a number of e-mail posts he has had with Caroni that assure the trip is all-expenses-included, they admit that it appears their captain has made an unfortunate mistake, but they are adamant. They suggest we call Caroni back in Paris to straighten things out, which we proceed to do.

We all go to the manager's hovel at the campground headquarters and dial the Land of Gaul. We get Caroni on the line and he asks to speak to me. Over a crackling phone line, the conversation goes something like this:

"Bon souis, Thierry," I begin.

"Bon souis Ole. Zere are zome problemz?"

"Not problemz. A misunderstanding."

"Yezz. But I told you at zee airport in Paree zat you must pay for zee fuel." Even if this were true, it's about a month too late for Walt.

"No, you did not say anything, at any time, about any fuel bill."

"Yez, I did."

"No, you did not." But there is little point in arguing. Thierry is there, in control of our finances, and I am here in the desert, a pawn in his game. The Frenchman has us over a barrel, this is the first time I ever found myself really disappointed with our host. I hang up and give Walt the bad news.

Walt is a very reasonable gringo. He is not worried about the thousand dirhams he must pay for both himself and his wife. He feels betrayed, but is determined to make the most of this journey, and to have a good time. He takes $200 from his hide-a-pocket and settles the bill. Caroni's staff are not exactly happy with the arrangement either, but they accept the cash with stonefaced goodwill.

Leg 3 Tazzarine to Morhid

Today we spend about two hours driving and flying to Morhid. Doctor Will assures me that we will be following a very beautiful valley called the Draa. We do, indeed, travel through a nice valley, but Will has overstated its splendor. We arrive in a nice hotel called Tuareg Oasis, about which we are pleased, after having spent last night at a campground in what the French call a 'bivouac'.

We go to some restaurant and eat the same dull food and drink the same syrupy mint tea as we have everywhere else. I am quickly becoming bored with this whole event. If I had not had the poor judgment of involving Walt and Rosilis in this event, I would catch the first bus to Marrakech, where I hope things would be better. Though the beauty and mystery of Morocco has been overstated and quickly worn thin, the call of Marrakech still intrigues.

I can't even get excited about the flying. Having just spent ten days hang gliding in México where the flying is awesome, inspirational and magical, I am jaded I guess. If I had to describe México in a hundred words or less I would be hard pressed. If I had to describe Morocco in a hundred words or less, I would just say 'it sucks' and leave it at that. A dreadful place. But I've got Walt and Rosilis with me and must make an effort to not bring them down. So far, they seem to be having more fun that anyone.

Leg 4 Tazzarine to Tata

We are rousted at 4:45 AM by Doctor Will with the prospect that we will travel a very bad road along the Algerian frontier. He is not lying. I experience a lifetime of off-road driving, compressed into one horrible morning, as Doctor Will exhibits a sado/masochistic tendency behind the wheel. Twice during this journey, he hits a rut so hard that the luggage in back cascades over the front seat and buries me.

Walt rides with us in the cat-cat for the first leg of the day's trip and flies the Clipper on the second leg. Will smashes and crunches the Mitsubishi, a sport-utility wagon, along the terrible road. He shows little respect for this vehicle or for the road, which is strewn with boulders and cut with dry washes. I consider what it must be like to drive the Paris-Dakar or the Baja 1000. I want nothing to do with it.

Algeria—care lose your head?

We drive in long periods of enforced silence. Talk, anyway, is out of the question without yelling. There is a constant smash and rattle of the cat-cat as it protests Doctor Will's abuse. I reflect, too, on the sanity of Jacques, the other Frenchman a quarter mile in front of us, who maintains the same punishing pace but is abusing his own cat cat—a Range Rover. At least Will drives a rental.

Which leads me to speculate about the scene at the cat cat rental agency in Casablanca where the Frenchies procured these vehicles:

"Bon jour monsieur. We are here to rent three cat-cats and beat the tar out of them in the desert."

"Of course, Sahib. Salam alaikum." *Peace be with you.*

We let Walt out of this punishment after the first leg of the day so he can fly the second leg, and we board Rosilis, who has just flown the first leg. We head out again, but this time, Praise be to Allah, we travel pavement. It's not far either, to Tata, but I arrive bone tired from having gripped my seat for hours.

Moroccan doughnuts

We stop for lunch, more of the flavorless orange-mush soup and some dubious sizzling meat, washed down with a Coke and some bitter coffee. We are brought to this night's hotel and we check in. There are no numbers on any of the room doors, no markings at all to identify the rooms, which I find peculiar, and which leads to some confusion. Walking to the lobby, I am approached by a guy all dressed up like John Travolta in GREASE, but that is where the similarity stops. He smiles at me through black teeth and gestures around at our humble surrounds.

"Eet iz berry gut, Allah akbar!" he declares in English.

"Huh?" I respond.

"Zee rooms, zee pool, zee sky!"

There are rooms, yes. There is a pool, too, but it looks badly in need of some chemicals and the water level is very low. The sky is nice, though, and so I agree.

"Allah Akbar!" I say, and he seems placated.

~ற≥ ≤ற~

"What strikes the most, is the total difference of manners between them and us, from the greatest object to the least. There is not the smallest similitude in the twenty-four hours. It is obvious in every trifle."
- Horace Walpole, Letters

~~~~~~~~~~~~~~~___~~~~~~~~~~~~~~

Leg 5 Tata to Taroudannt

The Doc and I leave as we do every morning, ahead of the fleet. We drive through pleasing countryside, mostly tight canyons and spare villages. The highway is one-lane blacktop, too narrow to pass without someone, usually both vehicles, pulling off onto the shoulder. We drive for about two hours and reach a point to stop and establish radio contact with the planes. Will has been instructed to wait here and confirm that all the planes have crossed the mountains.

Scrub 'em up, take 'em home to mama

As we wait, two mountain vixens, maybe sixteen years old, appear out of nowhere and hold at about fifty feet. They gawk and giggle at us as though we are quite the spectacle. They admire us with little shame, staring and laughing and pointing. They are quite spectacular themselves, covered as they are from head to toe in flowing robes, shawls, leggings and sandals. They have some sort of scarf swathing their heads. Red, orange, purple, pink, yellow and green, they are festooned like classy vocal parrots. The more fetching of the two re-arranges her turban-like headdress to reveal a little of her fine, if filthy, neck.

They stand there for some minutes, giggling and cooing all the while. Occasionally they squawk with glee. I try to approach, but for every step I consume, they put another between us like curious but wary birds. They laugh some more, and point shamelessly at us, finding us quite hilarious.

Finally, I decide to try some juggling, thinking to entertain them. But when I bend down and pick up three rocks from among the many scattered about, the birds suddenly seem threatened—as though the big stranger might actually try to stone them. They squeal and run several steps back. When I begin juggling they are not impressed, do not seem to think I am clever at all, but... they are somewhat relieved.

I try to get the cute one to agree to a juggling lesson, by holding out the rocks and using some sign language. But they are not interested and run from my approach. My guess is that I'm getting uglier all the time.

But they linger on, laughing hysterically at times, gesticulating and, of all things, sticking their tongues out at us. I find this display to be quite provocative. One of these birds has a serious overbite and is about as bowlegged as any woman I have ever beheld. The other is quite cute, in a peasant girl sort of way. In any event, their sense of style and mode of dress would make them tres chic on Haight Street in San Francisco.

Ultimately, they become bored with us, or our novelty wears off, or perhaps must keep some other assignation. I find myself disappointed when they leave, disappearing into the olive groves and desert.

~~~~~~~~~~~~~~~~   ~~~~~~~~~~~~~~~

Stronghold of the Berber women?

There is nothing out there, in the direction they take. Nothingness. They keep looking back at us and sticking their tongues out as they depart. A colorful duo, a delight to behold here in the desert, I have an urge to follow them and must reign myself in. How would I look, a dirty old man, following the young maidens to their desert stronghold? I would likely be beheaded. Next thing I know, they are gone.

~ℝ≥ ≤ℝ~

Sitting here in the desert, waiting the trikes to fly over, we discover that we have a flat tire. Then we discover that we also have a flat spare. These are circumstances that would normally cause only despair, but I find vindication of sorts: I predicted some days ago that we would end up with four flat tires if we keep driving around the desert on the thorny cactus you find hereabouts. When Doctor Will hears this prophecy he explodes;

"OH COME ON!" he hollers. "You have obviously never been off-piste!"

I don't know what kind of a gringo he thinks I am, but I have indeed been OFF-PISTE! I have been PISTE-OFF too for that matter, and I have seen cactus thorns cause flat tires, much as they have right now. But I must simply absorb the smug kidding he gives me in subsequent days while we await our first flat. Before long our tires must have been filled with thorns.

Now here we are—dead in the water. Or here I am, I should say, as the good doctor has departed with the tire on some rattletrap old truck that happened our way. He left me here with a bewhiskered old man in a polyester suit and a colorful knit beanie atop his noggin—a passerby, a wanderer, a desert nomad. A homeless bum? His suit has wide lapels with a dark ring around the collar, and though he lacks a tie, the old friend keeps the top button of his shirt neatly fastened, like maybe his mother dressed him. I try to strike up a conversation with the old peasant, and ask him several times if he speaks Español, and he nods affirmatively whenever I say "Español". I try to establish a link in that tongue, but to no avail. Although he nods and grins at everything I say, he utters nothing himself. Not a word.

He is a handsome old guy though, so I take another tack;

"¡YO JUAN!" I holler, and I pound my chest like King Kong. "¿SU NOMBRE?"

I try this in both Spanish and French. The old man nods and grins some more, but says not a word. Maybe I'm talking to a deaf man? I try again but I might as well be from Mars. I sing him a few bars of When You Wish Upon A Star, thinking maybe he's seen the movie. He laughs in surprise at this and seems delighted, but ultimately all attempts at conversation fail miserably, and we resign ourselves to wait in silent futility.

Mercifully, Doctor Will returns with the tire and we head out again, but not before the old man tries to bum a few dirhams from the gringo. Apparently, he was not satisfied with just my song—he requires cash. I give him a few dirhams, though I too, am nearly destitute. How to explain to an old man that you have no wealth when, quite obviously, as anyone can see, you do? Especially if you only speak Martian.

Soon we arrive at Taroudannt, The Ancient Walled City of the Flies. Well, perhaps the guidebooks don't call it that, ignoring, as they do, the flies, but this gringo cannot. The pesky vermin cover everything. We are delivered to our mid-day feast, which is more of the same boring fare with few surprises, and all of it covered with flies. There are French fries here; maybe the 'chef' has heard that we are mostly French. In any event we are served a mound of fried beef whose only virtue is that it is a tiny portion, piled high with fried potatoes. They are cold and so drenched in grease that they fall apart at the touch of a fork. Ronald McDonald would gag on this fare.

The food is getting worse, if possible, but the French are eating it stoically as though remembering all the while that before long they will be back on the Champs-Èlysées, dining on pâté de foie gras and confít de canard at Chez Pierre. They ignore the flies, which I find impossible. At any given moment I count six flies on the Frenchman seated across from me. Not until one pulls a landing on his nose does he even seem to notice, whatsoever.

Finally, disgusted by what I see, I remove myself from the scene, and go stand in the street. Here I find some relief from the flies, as there is a breeze coming in off the desert. But across the street is a butcher's shop, wherein hang several slabs of dead animal, also covered in flies. This sight, coupled with the realization that the few pieces of meat I did just manage to choke down may well have hung in that same window moments ago, renders me weak at the knees.

I turn from the doorway, seeking a more pleasant vista. The shop next door is the welder's shop. It is from here that originates the loud squalling of tortured machinery that has punctuated our lunch. The welder himself is grinding away happily on a bicycle sprocket. Sparks fly, and there is an incredible racket as both the sprocket and the grindstone protests the abuse.

The village welder must also be the local egg outlet, I surmise. Or maybe he just craves eggs. In any event, there are about fifty dozen eggs, in flats, perched atop his counter, in a column that stands head-high. The top flats are covered in shattered egg, as though a piece of re-bar, abundant in this shop, has fallen upon them. Bits of shell, a scramble of yolk and whites, litter the flats, the bench, and the floor. The flies are having an egg fest. It is just too much for this gringo, and I am about to bolt into the scorching desert.

I am relieved beyond words then, when the cat-cat is loaded with Frenchmen, to take us back to the hotel. I am the first to board.

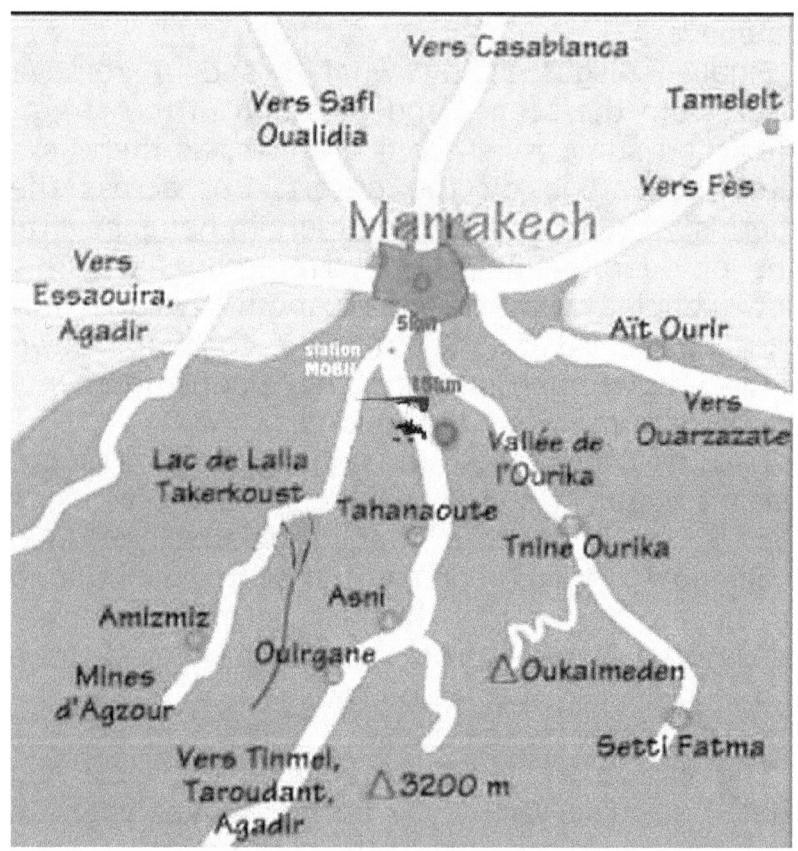

~ற≥≤ற~

Did ya know we're riding
on the Marrakech Express?
Do you know we're riding
on the Marrakech Express,
They're taking me to Marrakech!
All aboard the train!"
-David Crosby, Steven Stills and Graham Nash

On our Last Leg! Taroudannt to Marrakech

Another early morning with a long drive for the sawbones and myself, this time through the mountains. Out the window we have spectacular views of snow-capped mountains, stretching off into the distance. The doc never slows down to admire the view. We arrive at the outskirts of Marrakech and find a field where we think the trikes can land to end their journey. This is nothing more than a flat field, rocky, bisected by a couple of dirt roads. We are well in advance of the trikes, so when the doctor offers to take me to our hotel, I quickly accept the offer. I suspect he has become as tired of my company as I have of his. Neither of us wants to sit out here in the desert and listen to each other breath. So... off we go.

I am taken to Hotel Tropicana, deposited there with my luggage. There are many Germans at this hotel. Since it is around checkout time, they are boarding huge fancy busses for a journey of their own.

There is no room ready for me yet, so I sit in the lobby and have a short snooze. I awaken stiff and sore, so I stand up to stretch. I have a view of the pool outside and imagine my gleeful surprise when a German girl—a rather tall and well-endowed one at that—walks out poolside and strips off her shirt. She has delightful breasts, which spring free of their fetters.

A new day has dawned in Marrakech!

After a week in which every woman I have encountered has been swathed in robes from her very top to her very bottom, this is indeed a shock. The fraulein is clothed in nothing more than a tiny G-string and a tan!

My feet start moving of their own accord, and I drag my luggage out to the pool. Here I find women of all shapes and sizes, of all hues, all topless. There are tits everywhere: young ones, old ones, short ones, tall ones, skinny ones, brown ones! The big German's point slightly away from each other. She lays down on them next to a girl with lots of ribs. Her ass is now facing me, and it seems naked too, due to the G-string. I am astounded; I hide in the shade behind my reflective lenses, and admire the show. There are men here too, but they are easily ignored. I know this type of sun worshipping is common on the beaches of Europe, but I am shocked to find it in an Arab country.

The waiters here, all of them Arabs, seem to be a very happy bunch indeed and now I understand their glee. I wonder what kind of bribes must be paid to land one of these positions. Maybe you are born to the job, it's passed down from father to son?

Another French girl has just appeared. She is fully clothed, but near bursting from her blouse. She is accompanied by a gentleman with an enormous beer belly, and though she does not look happy, she graces me with a brief smile that is part grimace. I am overjoyed when she strips down to her G-string too, all bounces and wiggles. She sits with her tits aimed straight at me, as though they examine me with the same prurient intensity that I ogle them. She keeps her back to her escort, who does not seem to even notice her.

This show goes on for the better part of the morning until, disappointingly, clouds move in and shed a shadow on the display. Then, one by one, the women all don their frilly bras and sheer blouses, step into shorts and depart the pool, leaving me to ponder Life's mysteries.

My reverie is broken and I am removed from this little slice of Heaven when Doctor Will returns and informs me that we have chosen another hotel for our stay. My protests fall on deaf ears when I suggest we review this decision, and stay right here where the girls are just as naked, and as proud of it, as the iguanas that lounge hereabouts.

But tonight we are promised a Berber spectacular at a desert kasbah, and the Doctor has no patience for my desires.

I don't think I can stand much more excitement for one day, but if I am to be fed I must accompany my hosts. By eight o'clock we are all showered and ready to board the hotel bus for the quick ride into the desert, and a location called CHEZ ALI. The shower part is relevant, because my French companions have become a fragrant bunch, as if wanting to become as much a part of the local culture as possible. This would include the doctor who, although an American, has become quite Frenchy-fied, and does not seem to notice his own strong odor. Will has worn the same shirt all week long, and it has slowly changed color, like a lazy chameleon, from white to gray. He seems to have no luggage at all this doctor, only the emergency medical kit he brings along. But tonight we are a showered bunch, anyway.

We are whisked around the perimeter of Marrakech to the location of Chez Ali. This is a walled compound, designed to recall the fortified cities that here in Morocco are called 'kasbah'. Off the bus, we are paraded through an aisle of stern-faced and heavily armed Berbers on horseback. I cannot predict our future with any certainty... Will we be feted or run-through? Maybe that depends on our behavior tonight, but I can only hope that we will not be pitted against this bunch in any type of close warfare. They are a fierce looking assemblage.

Happily, we are met at the main portal by a Berber maiden, all decked out in gowns, and with some sort of silken crown atop her head, a gilded circlet that looks as though it may have a shoebox and coat hangar framework. It is draped with coins and tiny mirrors and rhinestones. Apart from a slice of her face, and her painted toes, all of which are covered with glitter, she is otherwise hidden in shapeless gowns.

She is our welcoming committee, and I think I just might be able to survive ten rounds with her.

As we pass the portal, we are made to pose with the mystery maiden for a photo. Later, during dinner, they will try to sell the photos to us for 200 dirham a pop.

We are escorted then into the keep, a large compound surrounding an open patch of ground where, I assume, the Berber Spectacular will later take place

The perimeter of this area is composed of maybe two-dozen private dining areas, one of which is reserved for our feast. I am disappointed when there are no hookahs. Marrakech is famous for its hashish. At least, I've always been convinced that the hashish was the main attraction for Crosby, Stills and Nash. Where is the hash?

Food is quickly laid at our table, more of the same tasteless orange soup, a pile of bread. The surprise tonight, is the carcass of half a lamb, slightly undercooked, which is unceremoniously tossed upon a platter with no thought whatsoever of presentation. Our waiter leans over the table and scrapes much of the meat from the bones with a fork, at which point this poor critter resembles nothing so much as roadkill.

The waiter, by the way, has a powerful body odor, which mingles with the ripe odor of the lamb, and causes me to lose what little appetite I arrived with. I am beginning to wonder if my olfactory system has not become super-sensitized, somehow.

There is the ubiquitous couscous, the likes of which I have been bored with since the first sample we had a week ago. There is the obligatory platter of oranges and bananas, presented as though it is a treasure.

I would prefer hashish.

I'm pretty sure these guys have a line on the hashish.

And... there is mint tea. The tea deserves mention, if only because it is the national drink of Morocco and much of the rest of the Arab world. Mint tea is served hot and with loads of sugar. It is so sweet it's nearly syrup. It is poured with some ritual into tiny glasses, until they are around half full, about one gulp. Sometimes, fresh mint leaves are added. If not, you would not know from looking if you are being served mint tea or, perhaps, a minty urine sample.

On one occasion, having grown weary of this brew, I insisted that our waiter dump the tea over a glass of ice. My logic was that a) I wanted a more refreshing beverage and b) the ice would cut the sugar as it melted. But this is more than our waiter can fathom. He stands over our table with a look of incredulous dismay, as though I have just asked him to pour the hot tea down my crotch.

He summons another waiter as a witness to our madness but together they cannot bring themselves to pour the tea over the ice. They summon the Maitre d'. This gentleman is dressed in a double-breasted suit that may once have belonged to Ricky Ricardo. He has an arrogant bearing, as a Maitre d' should, but a strong B.O., as a Maitre d' definitely should not.

After repeating our request to the captain, he surrenders to our directive with a resigned shrug of his shoulders and commands his crew that they should comply with the infidel's request. We wonder if we have not precipitated a small cultural revolution that will spread throughout Arabia.

ICED TEA!

During dinner at Chez Ali, we are set upon by one troop of Arab performers after another. They charge into our tent like some tiny but fierce invading army and scream and chant in our ears, until it is quite painful. One dancing maiden leans her face within inches of my ear and screams so loud and so shrill that my ear rings for the rest of the night. I could see her uvula vibrating. Meanwhile, the rest of the troop bangs a ragged rhythm on a variety of percussion-type instruments, a rhythm that I find does not enrich my dining experience, or relieve my mind of thoughts of the lamb carcass that has been left on the table. One performer bangs a piercing percussion on what looks like a brake drum from my old '53 Chevy station wagon.

Tomorrow is Walt's fiftieth birthday and some mention should be made of Walt and his wife Rosilis now. Since I convinced them that they should take this trip, that it would be a worthwhile experience, I feel somewhat responsible for their having a good time. I have no worries, though; Walt and Rosilis seem to be having more fun than anyone, in spite of Morocco. They have maintained their sense of humor and adventure throughout the trip, and often behave like new lovers. Rosilis has ordered a birthday cake for her man, which we await after the Berber Spectacular.

This Spectacular is held on the patch of dirt at center stage after the meal. It consists of all the strolling minstrels who had confronted us during dinner, the Mystery Maiden, and the Berber horsemen, too. While the former dance a dervish and raise clouds of dust, the Berber horsemen challenge us at full gallop from the far end of the pitch. They fire flintlock rifles charged with black powder. This causes a thunderous racket, and the air actually pulses with concussions. I am relieved when we are not pressed into hand-to-hand combat.

This continues for some time, then there are pyrotechnics and some other special effects, including a magic carpet ride, suspended across the grounds ala Ali Baba. But this is not Disney World; it looks fake. The Berbers have erected a pyrotechnic sign that they light afire: WELCOME TRANS SAHARA AIR MARATHON! it declares.

It seems like a bit of an exaggeration to me, but that's us!

After the drama, we return to the tent for Walt's birthday cake and more mint tea. The cake provides some diversion, because it is the most delicious chocolate cake I've ever had, a real surprise, even better than Mom's. Where did this come from? Why were we not served this in Beni Mellal, in Er Rachidia, in Tata and in Taroudannt?

It would have been even more delicious with a hashish appetizer.

Thus endth our Berber Spectacular, at least until the 'morrow when we are promised a pilgrimage within the walls of ancient Marrakech, founded by an Arab prince in 1065.

~◲≥ ≤◲~

I awaken parched and hungry, after the splendid Berber repast of the night before. Anticipating the first real breakfast since our arrival, I quickly head for the dining room. Certainly in a place as modern and extravagant as our current location there will be variety, perhaps even a menu, where I can make choices.

Alas!

I find nothing more than a long table awash in bread, butter and jelly, French style. The only difference from the last seven breakfasts I've had is the addition of platters of croissants. I am shocked and dismayed. Have not these people heard of Corn Flakes? Granola? Melon? French Toast? I eat what I can manage to wedge down and ponder the mysteries of this world, namely this:

The French, who otherwise may have the finest and most varied cuisine in the First World, eat bread and jelly for breakfast.

By 0930 hours we are paraded back onto the hotel bus for the Marrakech tour, for which we have all paid a hundred dirhams. I quickly become bored. We visit an aqueduct, an example of the one upon which Marrakech was founded in ancient times. This is a murky-brown pool, with giant carps that surface frequently for air. Then we go inside the walls of Marrakech and visit the Sultan's Palace. I suppose it is imposing and ornate, etc., but every piece of furniture or other embellishment has been removed as though the place was looted by thieves. All this has been replaced by a steady stream of tourists.

By the time we are off to visit some dead guy in his tomb, my boredom has become mixed with weariness. I would just catch a taxi back to the hotel, maybe stop off at the hotel Tropicana where the girls are naked, but I figure I should stick around for the souk. I will never be here again and I'd better see it while I can. Besides, the sky has become very gray today. The girls are probably not exposing themselves.

~ஶ≥ ≤ஶ~

Into The Souk

The souk is what the Moroccans call their market. If this souk is the grandest in all the Kingdom, as we have been assured, then I would hate to see a humble souk. Oh sure, there are all manner of goods for sale here, and absolutely nothing that appeals to me. Lots of brooms and mops and toilet fixtures and soap and shampoo and strange spices and fifty-pound bags of sugar and flour. Stacks of cassette tapes and barrels of olives.

 Olives everywhere, and bundles of mint leaves. Their cloying minty odor makes me wretch and gag. I suppose there is frankincense and myrrh too, buy I don't want any of it. The narrow streets and alleys of the souk are congested with mopeds, as are all the streets in Morocco—the national mode of transportation, I guess. I had no inkling of what a dreadful contraption is a moped until I encountered thousands of them here. Each one belches a foul stream of emissions, very irritating to the eyes, nose, throat and lungs. They observe no traffic laws, nor even those of common courtesy to pedestrians. Mopeds rule. Even more than the

mammoth diesel busses that inch through the tight streets, the mo-peds are awful.

The streets of the souk also appear to be filthy, a filth that has been piling up, removed and piled up yet again for centuries. I suddenly realize that I am adrift in a Sea of Shit. There is cat shit, dog shit, donkey shit, mule shit, horseshit and camel shit. Probably some other shit too, too shitty to mention. The air is malodorous of shit.

Combine this with the reeking smell of unwashed humanity, and the above-mentioned exhaust, and all of it confined by the walls of the surround, it is a heady environment. For a few moments I gag and I think I will add the odor of my own vomit to the mix, and maybe squeeze out some of my own shit too, but I catch a petite taxi out of the crush of humanity and order it back to the hotel, where the air is marginally better, and I can bath myself. Upon exit from the souk I drink in huge drafts of fresh air. So much for the souk- my first and last!

~ה≥≤ה~

Adios Morocco!

I awaken on my last day in Morocco and step out to the balcony of my hotel room. The distant snow-covered ridge that we have just flown around for a thousand kilometers—the High Atlas—has disappeared in a haze of smog, dust and humidity, leaving not so much as a trace of itself on the horizon. Just as all the mystique that had existed in my mind when I first came to Morocco has vanished in a disgusting haze, so has the High Atlas. I will be glad to get home.

I meet Walt and Rosilis for bread and jelly and we take a taxi to the airport. Along the way Rosilis

"¡Adios berbers!"

says grinning; "Walt had an interesting encounter with the shoe-shine boy last night."

"Oh yeah," I say. "What happened?"

"I stopped to have my shoes polished," says Walt. "I thought I'd spend a few of my last dirhams you know..." Rosilis giggled as he spoke.

"So?" I inquire.

"So I ask the kid how much for a shoeshine and he says five dirhams. I thought the price was negotiable. I didn't really care if my shoes were polished or not. I offer two dirhams..."

"And?"

"And we agree on three dirhams and so the kid polishes my shoes. But then when I pay him the agreed price, he says that it's three dirhams for each shoe!" Rosilis giggles some more.

"So what did you pay him?" I ask.

"Well I gave him three or four and walked off with just one shoe polished."

"The kid called him a Berber!" said Rosilis happily. She laughed then and hugged her man around the waist. "My big strong little Berber!" she sighed.

Mexican Rescue Squad or,
Fire On The Mountain

Walter found himself unable to fly, unable to sleep even, despondent over having lost his best friend Groucho. For twenty-three days in a row he would climb on his Honda 90 motor scooter early each morning and head out on the dusty trail, riding up this road and down that, poking his nose into every corner of that part of Mexico, passing out flyers with Groucho's likeness and asking everyone if they'd seen his dog.

The Mexicans thought the gringo had gone loco.

One evening on returning home to the airfield, saddle sore, tired and thirsty, he found that Chui Zaragoza was waiting for him. Chui was waiting in Walter's E-Z chair along with a couple of his amigos. Chui was poking on a liter bottle of cervesa Indio, and he was looking quite pleased with himself. Chui is an imposing figure; a tall, handsome Latino with broad shoulders, a swarthy complexion, and near-perfect teeth forming an immense smile. He was always well dressed and smelled strongly of after-shave. He never had a hair out of place. He was the youngest of eight Zaragoza brothers, but Walter found it impossible to disregard Chui Zaragoza even if, such as on an occasion like this when he was just weary and disappointed, he might have wanted to.

"Walter, nos encontramos de tu perrito," declared his big amigo as he stood to embrace the gringo. *We have found your little dog.* This was great news if true, but it didn't seem likely.

"¿Donde?" asked the gringo looking hopefully about. Groucho was nowhere in sight. If Chui has found Groucho, where is he?

"Arriba del monte donde lo perdiste," he replied. *Up on the mountain where you lost him.* This was bad information—Groucho had been lost at the bottom of the mountain, not the top.

"Lo perdí abajo del monte," Walter explained.

"Se subio buscando a ti," declared Chui confidently. *He must have climbed up there looking for you.* But Walter did not believe that Groucho had climbed the mountain looking for him for at least two good reasons. First—the gringo had ridden up the mountain himself when he realized that Groucho was missing, it must have been only about an hour after the fact. Groucho knew and loved the scooter and could pick the sound of that Honda 90 from all others. If Groucho had been anywhere atop the mountain when the gringo went looking for him he would have run to him...

¡Que lastima!

Secondly, there is no water atop the mountain, not a drop; it is a hot and dry place. But there is a nice cool river just below the mountain in the valley. Walter was sure that Groucho would have gone down the mountain, not up.

However... he was a desperate gringo and would listen to any ideas, however unlikely.

"¿Que mas?" he asked. *Is there more?*

"Groucho esta arriba y llore por ti," said Chui happily. *Groucho is up there and he's crying for you.*

"¿Por que llora Chui?" *Why is he crying?* Groucho was not a crying type of dog. He was not much of whiner or a yapper either. He would not even cry if you stepped on his tail because, well... he had no tail.

Chui shrugged his shoulders and observed the obvious; "Extraña de ti," he said. *He misses you.*

It was enough to make the big gringo himself cry, but Walter held his tears. How would it look to his Mexican amigos of he broke down in big giant sobs like he really felt inside? They would know he's lost his mind. It was pretty damn unlikely that Groucho was crying for him atop La Cumbre, but it sounded good.

"¿Porque no lo agarraste amigo?" he inquired. *Why didn't you grab him?*

"Tiene miedo," explained Chui. *He's scared.*

Now Walter knew Chui was really full of it. Groucho was a pet dog and he was not afraid of humans. Unlike the legions of Mexican stray dogs who are terrified of all people and scurry away from human contact, Groucho craved company. It was one of the things Walter loved him for—Man's Best Friend. Poor Groucho!

"No tiene miedo Chui. Es mascota," he said. *He's not afraid Chui. He's a pet.*

"¡Vamanos!" declared Chui. *Let's go!* With that, he stood and finished off the liter of beer, punctuated with a theatrical belch. He and his amigos were ready to swing into action for their sorrowful gringo amigo.

"¿Donde vamos?" inquired Walter, although he already knew the answer. He was following the Mexicans now, and they were headed for Chui's car.

"¡Hacia la cumbre!" they said in unison. *To the summit!*

As the gringo followed his amigos he recalled that "Chui" is a nickname for "Jesus". Maybe Chui would be his savior after all.

~௫≥≤௫~

Walter had never ridden in Chui Zaragoza's bad automobile, but he had seen it many times and heard it even more often. The vehicle was the baddest drag racing stock car in all of Mexico—no doubt. It was taking on all comers each Friday night out on the runway drag strip at the airfield, and it made a hellacious roar that had tormented Walter on countless sleepless nights. A large decal across the driver's side of the vehicle announced the name of the monster as "El Taliban". The decal also sported a very detailed likeness of US President George Dubyah, who was being slapped in the face by a bearded and turbaned mullah. To suggest that El Taliban was a bad vehicle was to understate the truth.

El Taliban was a 1979 Chevrolet Monte Carlo two-door sedan, with an enormous airscoop on the hood and numerous racing stripes and flames and decals. Across both flanks ran big block letters of the moniker turning into flames: *EL TALIBAN.*

Chui Zaragoza threw open the driver's door and gestured for all to pile in. They piled in through the driver's door because, for reasons unapparent to the gringo, the passenger side door had been welded shut. Probably a safety issue.

The seats in El Taliban had all been removed as well, with the exception of the driver's seat of course, for reasons that were quickly established by Chui's amigo Pedro who explained that the car is 'mas libianito' like that. *Lighter!* In any event, three dairy crates had been loaded in the car for their riding comfort, in place of the seats that had been installed in Detroit. Apparently the seatbelts had been overly cumbersome as well, because they were nowhere in sight either except for the driver, who had a five-point harness. Chui passed yet another crate through the door before hopping in himself, this one full of more of the one-liter bottles of Cervesa Indio that the Mexicans call "caguama". Nine more of them in fact.

Walter had mixed emotions about this latest cargo. On the one hand, he had fond memories of this beer—he remember landing his wing some years ago atop the pass to Toluca at something above ten thousand feet, where he was delighted to discover a tiny beer shack along the highway that sold nothing but cervesa Indio—a beer he had never tasted but which quickly became his favorite. He was very fond of cervesa Indio but he was not excited to have it in such quantity onboard the Taliban at that very moment, because it was a narrow windy mountain road they were about to navigate and his amigos seemed very thirsty. Gracias a Dios there was unlikely to be much traffic. In fact, after they left the highway to climb the peak, they were unlikely to meet anyone at all.

Chui Zaragoza slammed his door several times before he was satisfied with the results, and then touched the key that set El Taliban trembling with a ferocious growl and overwhelmed the gringo with an incredible roar, a roar that clogged his brain with trepidation, and a four-stroke vibration that shook him to his very soul. Chui stepped on the gas and popped the clutch and El Taliban lurched out of the airfield with a throaty snarl and a spray of gravel, knocking the gringo off his dairy crate and depositing him on the bare floor between Pedro's knees. As he drove, the driver peered in an unlikely manner over and around the giant airscoop on the hood. With one hand on the wheel he dialed the radio with the other, until he found a Mexican polka to fill in the gaps between the roars.

Darkness had fallen quickly as it will in the tropics, and the night was pitch-black as the rescue party turned off the paved highway and on to the steep cobblestone trail to the summit. Chui and his amigos were happy to be helping out the gringo and cranked the tunes to a painful and distorted volume to demonstrate their enthusiasm.

"¿Cuanto costo el perro?" asked Pedro. *How much did the dog cost?*

"No costo nada," the gringo explained. *He didn't cost anything.* This news was met with incredulous stares that said, *If the dog didn't cost anything, why the big worry?*

"¿Es macho o es embra?" came the next query. They were always the same questions when it came to Walter's dog, first: how much did it cost and then, is it male or is it female.

"No es macho ni es embra," Walter replied. *He's neither male nor female.* To embellish this point, which the Mexicans otherwise would just not understand, the gringo held up two fingers and wagged them open-and-closed in a scissors-like motion to indicate that Groucho's huevos had been removed. "Era macho," he explained. *He was male...*

This news caused dog-like howls of anguish while Walter's amigos all clutched for their own huevos, as though perhaps the gringo might just whip out a pair of hedge clippers and threaten them all with vasectomies or worse...

Castration.

Disfiguration.

It was with some relief then when El Taliban reached the top of the mountain road where Walter had been hucking himself off the cliff for a dozen years or so. He was quite happy when Chui shut down El Taliban, not just for the blessed respite from the horrible racket created by spurring the beast up the steep rocky road, but also because of an acrid smoky smell of burned rubber or wiring or something, which seemed to be emanating from under the dash. He spilled out of Chui's wagon with the rest of the gang and gulped in some fresh air.

It was strange to be up here in the darkness, the lights of Old Colima town twinkled warmly down below. Chui turned off the music and insisted everyone be still. Suddenly all was quiet atop La Cumbre. He ordered the gringo to call for his perrito. "Andale," he said.

Feeling a bit ridiculous, but very desperate too, Walter complied.

"¡GROUCHO!" he hollered.

...nothing...

"¡GROUCHOOOO!" louder this time.

...still nada...

Walter walked carefully around the top of the mountain as his eyes adjusted to the darkness, yelling and hollering like a danged fool gringo. He whistled as he had so many times for Groucho, and yelled himself hoarse, but all for naught. There was no Groucho.

The sorry gringo returned to El Taliban where his amigos were poking most happily at the caguama bottles of cervesa Indio. Chui insisted he climb high up the ladder on the old cathedral that sat atop the peak, and although Walter felt a bit of a sinner, he climbed up the ladder as high as he dared, hollered and whistled some more. But it was no good. Groucho was not atop the mountain. Just as Walter had confirmed that first terrible day and just as he feared all along...

Groucho was gone.

Dejected, the rescue party climbed back into the racecar and set sail down the hill.

It was about halfway down the mountain when the situation went critical. Suddenly, thick smoke and then flames leaped from under the dash and the headlights went out, plunging the World into sudden and complete darkness.   Except for the small Purgatory of sparks and yellow flames inside the vehicle, everything was dark as Hell.

"¡Sále, sále, sále!" barked the gringo. *Get out, get out, get out!*

El Taliban lurched to a rumbling halt as he was swept with panic. Flames were all he could see, as though he had ridden El Taliban to Hell and Damnation. Flames, and Chui's demented grin that is, like some awful latino Cheshire gato. Walter was confused for a moment—was he with Dante in his Inferno, or with Alice in her Wonderland?

Fortunately, his Mexican amigos had a solution at hand, because they calmly passed a caguama of cold cervesa Indio to Chui Zaragoza. The big Mexican gave the bottle a good shake or two to set the contents to fizz, and then deftly popped the lid with a Bic cigarette lighter. The resultant spew of fermented hops made quick work of the fire and the damnation too. Within moments the flames had been extinguished and nothing but a pall of plastic smoke filled El Taliban. Chui was clearly relieved, there were even a few swigs left in the bottle to quench his thirst.

There still seemed to be more smoke coming from under the hood though, so the rescue party all clambered out of El Taliban once again and Chui threw open the hood. A small hot-spot on the firewall drew the driver's attention and was quickly doused with yet another spray of the tasty suds. Soon the three amigos were heads-down under the dash, making the necessary repairs to the frazzled wiring. It was not long before the search party returned safely to the airfield.

Sadly, they never did find Groucho. They never

even heard Groucho crying. It seemed quite unlikely that Groucho was atop the mountain after all. The whole experience had left Walter disappointed and uh, rather stinky.

But it was the night the gringo learned to recognize a Mexican fire extinguisher when he saw one, and how to use it.

From Three Kings To The Pulqueria or,
A Mexican Bargain

Walter unloaded the gliders from the Ford-From-Hell and contemplated the day's flying. Today had been a flight leaving the resident—house—thermal at El Peñon del Diablo and heading for Los Tres Reyes—three volcanic lava domes that jut into the sky in the neighboring state of Michoacan, pretty much in the middle of nowhere. At Tres Reyes, the object had been to climb out to such altitude to glide to an imposing rock wall named El Divisadero, and arrive there with altitude sufficient to climb out in that house thermal, to an altitude sufficient to downwind all the way home to Valle de Bravo and land at the beach.

Walter didn't really want to make the flight under the circumstances: he had eight New York pilots in tow and felt rather responsible for their well-being. Not to mention that they would all be flying Walter's gliders; expensive equipment actually belonging, for the most part, to Kenny Brown and Pacific Airwave. Walter knew there was a high probability that of the seven New Yorkers who wanted this flight, at least one or two would fail to complete it and land in some distant field of 'milpa' and be very lost, maybe lost forever. They would be down in a very mountainous land, in a labyrinth of sketchy dirt roads and where no one speaks Ingles.

He realized his concern was, for the most part, for his equipment, which he could ill afford to lose. But he wasn't about to tell his amigos that. The New York pilots had come to Mexico for bitchin' winter thermals, but also for Adventure. Flying from

El Peñon, in the Estado of Mexico, and sinking into neighboring Estado de Michoacan, would indeed qualify as an Adventure. If it all went to hell, perhaps 'Nightmare' might better describe the Adventure.

Los Tres Reyes—the Three Kings

After much peer pressure Walter had capitulated and planned the flight for the following day.

They were a colorful bunch, these New Yorkers, and they confounded the notion that all New Yorkers are obnoxious. Very enthusiastic pilots, they were also mostly quite experienced. With the exception of Chuck Bell (Carlos Campana) they all were old leather, having flown many sites for many years. Carlos made up for his inexperience by returning not once or twice to fly Mexico—in the same season—but three times. The leader of the bunch was Paul Voight of Fly High Hang Gliding in Pine Bush, New York. Pablo and Walter had sat down to breakfast at a fly-in in Telluride, Colorado some years prior to this flight and Walter had talked him into arranging groups of pilots for flying tours in the Mexican highlands. There was also Bill Jolly and JJ LaMarch and BoBo. Linda Castle, female pilot extraordinaire, had somehow appeared at Walter's hotel and joined the group. Several local Mexican pilots had thrown their wings atop the Ford and Chocho—Walter's driver—completed the bunch. The Ford had made slow but steady progress up the long dusty road to the sky.

Now, here they stood on launch at El Peñon, kicking dirt to check the wind. Walter untied the gliders and pulled his own off the top of the stack. Then he joined the New Yorkers on launch while the local Mexican pilots busied themselves with setting up.

"Let's go gringos!" hollered Walter at his bunch. They were all doing what they were conditioned to do back in New York upon arrival at launch—they were kicking up dirt to watch the dust and try and determine how the conditions were at launch. The locals knew better. "You don't see the locals wasting time kicking dirt do you?" He pointed back into the trees where the locals were already spreading wings and stuffing battens. "You guys gonna fly or farm?" he inquired. The New Yorkers were not farmers, but they stood on launch gazing at the sky. Cumulus clouds were forming about a mile or more above them, and Mexican buzzards circled overhead. Launch would take place around 13:30 hours and there was plenty of work to do to be ready on time. As leader, Pablo spoke for the whole group:

"Looks a little strong today Bwana." Pablo called Walter 'Bwana' because he was in charge. "Maybe we should watch the wind a little."

Walter pointed over his head at the clouds forming there. They floated in the sky without so much as a hint of movement.

"Ain't no wind at all Pablo," he observed. "That's the house thermal you feel and, yes, it is strong. In fact, it is kick-ass. Would you prefer I take you somewhere with whimpy thermals?"

The New Yorkers craned their necks and turned their attention back to the clouds. One by one they confirmed what Walter had said and turned their faces back to launch.

A buzzard was making a low pass at eye level and being rocked in the strong turbulence in front of the slot in the trees that was launch. A collapsed volcanic crater dominated the valley below and they all stood in the pine forest atop its rim, wondering what the chingada to do. In the near distance towered an extinct volcanic lava dome christened El Peñon del Diablo—The Rock of the Devil.

Another thermal came roaring through launched and swayed the trees. Carlos grabbed for his hat but too late; the thermal swiped it off his noggin and sent it flying into the trees behind launch. The New Yorkers stood with jaws agape and Walter pointed back into the trees where the locals were already tensioning cloth and frames. He needed to spur them into action.

But before he could speak there came a loud *crack* from below launch that grabbed the attention of one and all—it sounded something like a shotgun blast. A large old pine had stood on that mountainside for centuries, but not today. Today the thermal gods had come for it. As the gringos, watched the force-of-wind in the thermal split the old trunk wide open, and sent it smashing to the launch slope with a horrific crash. Squirrels, lizards and birds ran and flew off in a panic while dust, debris and bits of bark were swept up launch with the wind.

Evertbody grabbed their hats now; the New Yorkers turned to Walter with a look of terrified wonder. The Mexicans had also heard the commotion and came running from the forest.

"¿Que le pasó?" *What happened?* inquired Santiago. He'd flown here as much as anyone and Walter always valued his judgment with regard to El Peñon.

"El arbol se caio con el viento," said Walter, pointing with a finger. *The tree fell with the wind.*

"¿De veras?" said Santi. *Really?* "¡Uhh hoo hoo!" he continued with a wicked grin. "Seria muy cabron today!" He laughed and turned with a happy rush back into the trees, yelling at his amigos, "¡Se caio un arbol, se caio un arblo!"

"What's that mean, moo-wee-kay-brone Bwana?" asked Pablo.

How could Walter explain? *It's going to be very goat today?*

"He means, let's stop buttin' around and quit with the kickin' dirt and get those wings set up; times a-wasting. We launch in forty-five minutes. Let's go gringos! Vamanos!"

~ៗ≥≤ៗ~

Soon all pilots had launched successfully and were circling out in the strong lift over launch. Santiago knew what he was talking about; the thermals were strong—*muy cabron*. Walter was torn between leading the group or bringing up the rear. He also had to concentrate on his own flying to avoid sinking out himself, which would be the ultimate indignity.

But the Mexican skies came through that day and all the pilots who departed for Los Tres Reyes actually managed to get there and work their way back up to cloudbase. For a while they circled the clouds far above a dusty hamlet called San Pedro de Tanayác. With much excited chatter over the two-way radios, the New Yorkers and the locals had a ball, tiny dots in the big Mexican blue.

Onward they flew towards El Divisadero, a microwave station atop a precipice looking west over impossibly rough terrain—now gazing out over a village called El Zacazonapan. Working the lift that rises from the imposing granite wall, all pilots returned to cloudbase for the long downwind glide into Valle de Bravo and the safety of home. One by one they circled the landing area or worked some scattered lift over town as though reluctant to end the journey.

Walter felt the glow of joy and satisfaction of all his arriving pilots as they turned base-leg and dove on in for landing.

The Ford arrived with a cooler full of cervesa and, drinking one, Walter watched his pilots land in the gentle lake breezes and felt as though he was the luckiest gringo in the entire World. *They pay me to do this!*

~~~~~~~~~~~~~~~~~~~~~~_____~~~~~~~~~~~~~~~~

The flyers bagged the gliders and were soon quaffing chilly cervesa around the Ford-From-Hell. Some other pilots who had launched later in the day came floating in to land and were judged for style. Pablo turned to Walter.

"How the hell do you top that act Bwana?" he asked. "We'll have to do something special tonight. We can't just eat and drink like the rest of the nights here. We wanna celebrate. That was one of the most awesome experiences of my life!"

This seemed to be the general consensus among the crowd; something else remarkable would have to happen on this day.

"Whatcha got in mind Pablo?" Walter asked. He was quite happy to just eat and drink like the rest of the nights. He should have kept his mouth shut.

"What about that little cantina we pass on the way to the mercado?" said Bobo. "You know—that funky little hole-in-the-wall that looks interesting. What say we stop in there for a drink and then head to dinner?"

The lawyer from New York was referring to the pulqueria, a locals-only watering hole favored by the peasant class when they wanted to really tie one on. There always seemed to be a passed-out drunk just meters from the door, flies buzzing his head, dogs hanging out nearby. Just the other day as Walter walked past the pulqueria, one ugly cur had actually arisen briefly to walk over to the day's drunk and sniff him a moment, then lift his leg and piss on his inert form. Walter figured this was a Mexican dog's opportunity just too good to pass up. The drunk had not so much as varied the rhythm of his snoring.

"You boys wanna go to the pulqueria Bobo? We got nice bars and discos with fresh señoritas here. The pulqueria doesn't qualify for either. Let's not and say we did."

"It's the experience, Bwana. The true Mexican experience we long for. A little real-life Mexican culture, rub elbows with the commoner." This came from Paul—the leader of the bunch. Pablo had taken to Mexico with alacrity, and was enthusiastically swilling cervesa. "If you won't take us were goin' in by ourselves. Right amigos?"

This was met by nods and grunts of approval, although no one in the group looked as committed as Bobo.

Walter thought he'd try at least once to head off this idea before it blossomed into action; the pulqueria was known to be a rough place, even as cantinas go. "Do you guys even know what pulque is?" he asked. They all stood blankly, awaiting an explanation. So Walter continued: "Pulque was discovered by the ancient Actec King Quetzalcoatl— Feathered Serpent—who commissioned his clerics to invent a sacred tonic for his warriors."

This was a bit of an exaggeration, but it sounded good, so Walter continued... "Pulque, for your information, was created quite by accident when an maguey cactus was hacked open and allowed to rot in the sun until it started to stink." Walter was digging this culture stuff. He was the guide after all—he could say pretty much whatever he liked. "When the King's men were forced to swill the resultant slime, they became quite hysterical and fell about comically—likely the first drunks in the New World.

~~~~~~~~~~~~~~~_____~~~~~~~~~~~~~

"The King then decided this was a Divine Message, and ordered full-scale rotting of maguey cactus. Pulque—pulp—was one of the first natural spirits mass-produced in the New World and production has changed little in the subsequent centuries. 'Pulque' is rotten cactus with the consistency of phlegm and the flavor of vomit. You gringos still want to give it a try?"

"They serve cervesa there too!" said Bobo, "I

saw one on the bar when I poked my head in there."

"I'll give anything a try once," said Carlos. "Even slimy cactus juice! I say... pulqueria!"

"¡Pulqueria, pulqueria, pulque...!" The chorus was taken up by all the gringos, and several passers-by looked askance at them, as though they had quite lost their collective minds.

Gringos?

In the pulqueria?

There was little Walter could do but give in to peer pressure and plan to visit the pulqueria. He was only the guide after all; he would have to join them just to keep them out of trouble.

~ℕ≥ ≤ℕ~

That evening they all met in the Zocalo, the central square you find in any Mexican town, where the locals gather to socialize. The New Yorkers were all there looking sunburned and windblown. Linda Castle had come along too—looking out-of-place in tight jeans and t-shirt. Walter had an urge to throw a colorful baggy dress like the Mexican women wore over her, but Linda was too hot for that. She asked the guide if they allowed women in the pulqueria. Walter said he thought so but that might depend on what kind of woman. It was clear to see even from

outside in the street that they had allowed some women in—pinups on the dusty walls. Linda was determined to stick with the group though, so they all headed en mass down the dusty alley towards the bar.

Arriving at the swinging door, Walter noticed a foul vomit odor, which he knew actually came from the pulque itself. Throwing open the door, he let Bobo enter first. After all, this was his big idea. The gringos followed one by one until all had shuffled in. There were many old Playboy centerfolds on the wall and a large dusty mirror over the bar. The mirror had an impact crack, which fanned out from about head high as though a head had indeed impacted there some time ago. All faces in the dingy place turned one by one to see the commotion at the door and as they saw the gringos, all faces registered shock or disgust.

¡Gringos!

¡This was no place for gringos!

Let them have the discos and restaurants..

¿But the pulqueria?

¡Nunca jamas!

A hush fell over the crowd.

Someone shut off the musica and a raucous Mexican polka died abruptly.

A scraggly old hound dog lifted his head off the barroom floor, stood suddenly, and cleared out through the back door as though fearful of a fight.

Walter wondered how to diffuse the situation. A long second passed before he felt a motion at his side and noticed Linda, poking her head over Walter's shoulder to survey the scene. Linda is an attractive blonde gringa, beautiful really, much like the pinups over the bar. Although she, of course, was quite fully clothed. But suddenly Walter had an inspiration...

If that's what they like, let's give it to 'em, he decided.

Stepping aside in the tight quarters Walter brought Linda forward a half step and suddenly all eyes within the pulqueria focused on her. A low mutter of surprised approval rose from within the dingy dungeon of drunkenness, along with a couple of soft wolf-whistles. Before things could get out of hand Walter figured he needed the upper-hand.

In the best Español he could muster he called out a saying so all could hear, a Mexican proposition that was new to him but seemed fitting at the moment: "Venimos," he yelled, "cambiar esta muchacha para dos llantas buenas!" Walter had heard this expression just the other day at the auto parts store and liked it and practiced it in his head over and over until he knew he had it right. He liked it and hoped someday he'd have the chance to use it to good advantage but he never thought his chance would come so soon.

Or be so right...

Well, if that didn't galvanize the situation! In the next moment the pulqueria erupted into a chaos of cheers and shouts. Chairs and tables were shoved aside and places offered and someone stuck a cervesa in Walter's hand without even asking. The jukebox was sparked to life and the volume cranked. Where just moments ago you could have heard a pin drop, now all was happy pandemonium. It certainly seems like the desired reaction, that the right words had been said after all and, pleased with the results, Walter now went for broke:

"Cervesa para todos!" he yelled to the bartender, who leaped into action with a silly grin.

"¡A sus ordenes señor!" he called. If Walter wasn't mistaken, he showed a happy look of relief too. In the next few minutes all the gringos and all the paisanos wore the look of old friends and began to pour down the beer and generally make merry.

A small but critical crowd gathered around Linda and scrutinized her with approving eyes. Over his shoulder Walter could see Bobo bellied up to the bar and being served the slimy swill called pulque from a barrel.

As Walter watched, Bobo sniffed and made a face and then; to the glee of his newfound friends he bravely swilled the swill.

Linda's eyes bugged as she buried her face in her guide's back. "Walter, Walter," she inquired. "Are those guys over there really... Oh God... are they pissing?"

Walter followed her glance with his eyes and, sure enough, the entire place it seemed, was surrounded by an elongated urinal/spittoon/swill trough, inclined slightly downhill to carry the contents away into the gutter. This behavior may well have explained the conspicuous absence of women in the pulqueria—there were only Linda and the pinups.

As Walter watched, an old piasano turned his back on the bar, stood at the trough and took a leak, then shook himself dry and put it away. With that chore done he turned back to the bar and his refreshments.

Linda had seen enough. With a glance that said *I'm outta here!* She turned for the door, but Walter was too quick and caught her elbow before she could depart.

"Whoa whoa whoa now! You can't go anywhere. Without you we'd probably be havin' our collective asses kicked at this very moment. You stay here 'till we can all make a timelier exit. I want us all out safely."

"Whacha mean without me? What'd I have to do with anything?"

"Didn't you hear the announcement I made there when things were so tense?"

"So...? What was that all about anyway?" Linda twisted her arm out from Walter's grasp to break free. But she stood still long enough to hear his explanation.

"I made them an offer they just couldn't refuse," said Walter. "I told 'em we've come to trade this woman for two good tires!" Linda gasped and then scowled at Walter. She glanced warily at the crowd, sizing 'em up. They were still sizing her up too...

"Ain't a one here can catch me!" she said and she was right. Linda is a gorgeous gringa and a fast one too. Fleet like a deer, she spun on her heel for the door. Walter let her go this time, despite loud objections from the bar. *We'll have to make it up to her on some other occasion he thought—she's a good sport.*

He turned back to the bar with a shrug of his shoulders. The anger was forgotten now, and Pablo was downing a pulque to the delight of all. His eyes bulged in disgust, but he got it down the hatch, and handed the cup to Walter.

Flight Of Pelicano Uno or, Mexico Bound Again

A pickup truck sped up the drive in a large cloud of dust. It had Mexican plates on it—from the Estado de Sonora. Out jumped Alfredo. When Alfredo appeared at the hangar door a general sigh of exasperation went through the barn.

"Here he comes again."

Whenever Alfredo show up was a good time to leave.

The big Mexican would need parts—and lots of them. That, in itself, was no trouble; we had lots of parts. In fact, we were there to sell parts, trikes and instruction. Parts sales were good. But our parts were expensive and Alfredo always needed more parts than he could pay for. When Alf arrived there would be lots of pulling parts off the shelves and before he left there would be lots of putting parts back on the shelf. That's how it worked with Aflie.

I was the Mexico specialist though, and I was always glad to see my amigos from south-of-the-border, if nothing else it gave me a chance to hone my Español. Besides, if he had come all this way we were likely to sell him something.

"¡Hola amigo!" I called as Alfie strode through the hangar door. "¿Y este milagro?" It was the standard greeting when two friends meet who haven't seen each other in ages. *And this miracle?*

About fifteen years earlier Alfredo had been standing on a tiny runway outside of Hermosillo, Sonora flying his radio-controlled airplane when someone said, "¡Mira—ultraligero!" *Look—an ultralight!*

At about that same moment I was flying along in my trike outside of Hermosillo wondering what to do with myself when I looked down and there was a tiny RC strip.

We had all been surprised when I chopped the throttle and dove on in. Alfredo and I have been amigos ever since, and I like to think they saw the gringo as poco loco. *A little crazy.*

So now my amigo gave me a big abrazo in the Mexican way, approaching me with arms wide and then embracing me and slapping me on the back three times, ending with an endearing squeeze. It's a salutation that takes some gettin' used to for most gringos.

"Que gusto ver te," said my amigo. *How great to see you.* "¿Como haz estado?" *How have you been?*

I had been fine and so I told him. He gazed around the hangar and whistled softly at all the bitchin' flying machines that we had stacked in there. We could stack a baker's dozen trikes in there—if we had Greg do the stacking—and that's what Alfredo was looking at.

"¡Que maravilla!" he declared. *Marvelous!*

"¿Cuantos quieres?" I asked jokingly. In all my years at the Ultralight Flight Center of the Universe I had never seen Alf buy a trike, he was all about buying them used and cheap and repairing or rebuilding them but today he had a surprise in store for us.

"Quiero solo uno," he replied. *I just want one.* His eyes fell upon a brand-spanking new Air Creation Tanarg—the fanciest and priciest flex-wing aircraft in the sky—that was sitting on the hangar floor still wrapped in the cellophane that it was shipped over here from Europe in. The cellophane wrap was left on her to keep the desert dust and the occasional bird guano off the paint job, and to show everyone that she was indeed new. Alfredo strode over to it and whistled once again. He was looking at sixty-thousand-dollars worth of trike—the first such expensive machines that we had ever heard of, a luxurious wagon with a Rotax 912 four-stroke engine, automatic-lift system for the wing, adjustable seats with leather upholstery, high-performance wing and too many other options to list here. We had taken delivery on six of these new trikes, shipped across the pond in a sea container, five of which had been sold even before they arrived. What Alfredo was looking at was the only one left from that order—the only one still wrapped like a Christmas present. It was red, it was fancy, it was pricey, it even smelled new.

"Tomo aquel," he said. *I'll take this one.*

Of course, I thought my amigo was pulling my pierna. In fact, I wasn't sure I'd heard him correctly, maybe it was a translation error.

I'll take this one...?

Alfredo didn't buy sixty-thousand-dollar cars let along trikes. "Ha!" I said with a grin.

"En serio," he replied. He whipped a check from his shirt pocket and handed it to me. *I'm serious.*

I took the check in hand and examined it carefully. It was written for twenty-five thousand dollars even, drawn on the Bank of Phoenix, a signature was scrawled across it. It was from some outfit called Groupo Peñasco and showed an address in Mexico but the bank wasn't. Apparently,

Groupo Peñasco wanted a trike and they'd sent Alfredo to pick one out. He stood there now and grinned back at me and asked, "Es disponible? *Is it available?*

"Hijo de la puta," I said softly, which caused Alfredo some mirth. *Son of a whore!*

I turned and took two steps stage right and slid open the office door. Alfredo and I stepped inside the cool of the office and walked over to John's desk. He was sitting in his chair in front of his computer and did not seem too excited about my entry with the Mexican tagging along. He probably figured Alfredo was going to be his usual parts nuisance.

"Hola amigos," he offered.

"Juanito..." said Alfredo and extended his hand. There was no giant Mexican abrazo because Juanito remained seated in his chair.

"Check it out," I said, and I handed him the check. Juan's eyes scanned it for a moment and he said,

"Cool. What's this for?" he waved it in the breeze of the air conditioner, like maybe it was too hot to hold.

"For that Tanarg out there." I replied.

"The Tanarg?" said Juan. His face wore a vacant look—the idea was so foreign to him.

"Yeah," I clarified. "The one still in its wrapper."

"He want's that Tanarg?" said Juan. Then he looked at Alfredo. "You want that Tanarg?"

"Si señor," came the reply. "Eff eez afailabull."

Juan looked us over for a bit while the reality settled upon him. He scrutinized the check again, now that it had cooled a bit in his fingers. Then he was smiling at us.

~~~~~~~~~~~~~~~~_____~~~~~~~~~~~~~~

"Hot damn," he said. "You betcha it's available. Congratulations!"

"Dees ees dee deposito," said our amigo. "I bee bak wid the res when ees ready. Bueno?"

"Bueno," replied Juan, standing now. "We'll have it ready in a week or two at most. I'm actually waiting for a few details from the factory but it's flyable just like it is. All we need to do is unwrap it really. Set up the wing and such. Bolt on the prop. Test-fly it."

We stood there grinning at each other for a moment then Alf said, "Tiene radio?" *Does it have a radio?*

"Optional," replied Juan. "You want a radio, we'll get you a radio."

"Porsupuesto," agreed Alfredo. *"Of course."*

Juan shoved back his seat and we all made a bee-line for the new trike. Stepping from the office into the hangar John said, "Hey Greg, order up a radio for this here Tanarg would ya? Looks like we've got it sold."

Greg turned from his task at the workbench with a surprised look on his face. "Oh yeah?" he asked. "Who bought her?"

"Alfredo here just put down a deposit. I'm headed to the bank to deposit his deposit. He's gonna need a radio."

"One moor ting," said Alfie. "Un condición."

"What's that now?" asked Juan.

"Tenemos que entregar lo a Peñasco," he said. I was not sure about that word—*entregar.* "Bueno?" he asked.

"Entregar?" asked Juan y yo in tandem. "Que es 'entregar'?" *What's it mean—entregar?*

"Deelibere," said Alfie. "Fly. We muz fly eet zere." To demonstrate to the gringos, as though we might be a little slow with such matters, Alf embellished with a bit of hand-flying. "Zoom!" he said. "First we buy eet, zen we fly eet zere!"

"Of course!" said Juan and I together like a cheer. "Entregar!"

"I don't see any problem with that." It was John talking now, and he was looking right at me. As the local Mexico expert, as the only one of us gringos who had ever flown across the border into Mexico, as the only one foolish enough to fly across the border, or even contemplate such a thing, the job would fall to me.

Alfie too looked at me now. "Voy contigo," he said. *I'll go with you*

With that, it was agreed.

Frankly, I could have jumped out of my hide. I had not flown a trike in Mexico since the Good Old Days, back when I used to just load the contraption with so much gear the little 503s we had back then would barely lift it, and then I would hop in and go. Also, I needed a bit of adventure about then as I had become far too sedentary. Plus—I would get to fly the fancy wagon after all. I was tingling as I stood there in the hangar and we all gazed at the trike. It looked like Adventure.

"Bueno," said Alfie. "¿No Tienes hambre?" *Okay. Aren't you hungry?*

Juan was picking up on this Español stuff and knew that much. He pulled out his wallet and handed me a few bills. "Why don't you guys go over to the café and enjoy yourselves... Have a burger and a few beers," he offered. "I'm buyin'. When I get back from the bank we'll unwrap that baby, maybe set up a new wing."

~₪ ≥ ≤ ₪~

Two weeks later Alfredo and I arose well before the sun and began to suit-up for our flight. We had a brand-new trike and wing with brand-new helmet-comms and brand-new flight suits. I don't know if my amigo felt quite as brand-new as I did that morning, but it was surely a new day.

"I taak dee front," said my amigo when it came time to climb aboard. The whole hangar crowd had gathered for the big day. John was taking pictures and Greg was topping-off the fuel and even Julie had gotten up early for this occasion. Alfredo, it seemed, wanted the front seat so he could fly in Gringolandia—something he had never done before.

"The sky is the same here as in Mexico," I told him and climbed in the back seat.

~~~~~~~~~~~~~~~~~~~~~~~~~~~~

"Just keep out of Luke," said Juan sagely. Luke Air Force Base would be our first obstacle—we would need to stay low and fly around their airspace if we did not want to get shot down.

"I know the way boss," I said. "Don't you worry none." I had already received the lecture from John about what a big responsibility this was and how important our success was. Of course, I already understood that but Juan had to tell me anyway.

"Call the gunnery range too."

"Right-o boss. When we land at Gila Bend. We'll swap seats there." As much as Alfredo wanted to fly in the States, I wanted to fly in Mexico.

Alfredo climbed aboard and we went through the start-up sequence and with a wave 'adios!' we dropped the brakes. The Tanarg started to roll and we were on our way. A glance at the hour meter on the dash showed the Tanarg had just one point one hours total time...

~ロ≥≤ロ~

Alfredo had purchased the fancy trike for a rich guy in Puerto Peñasco, Sonora, Mexico—a place known to many gringos as Rocky Point. The rich guy just wanted it for fun; he was one of Alfredo's students and he was going to hangar it and fly it there, with dreams of flying it to Tierra Del Fuego some day. Our objective was simply to pilot it to the airfield in Peñasco and tuck it safely in the hangar, but there were a few complications.

It was going to be easy to get past the facility at Luke. I had made this flight many times. The flight from there to Gila Bend Municipal Airport (E63) was going to be fabulous. We would be flying the flatlands and we were to be flying early on a winter's morning and we were looking at smooth cool air. But after Gila Bend things got a bit dicey. I pointed Alfredo along the way and soon the strip hove into view. Alfredo flew a pattern while I called our approach from the back seat but there was no other traffic and so we set down and taxied over to the terminal. It was deserted and rather decrepit too... In the way of civil aviation in the Cradle of Aviation in the last few years of the 20th century, almost nobody flew.

We shut down the motor and climbed out to relieve our bladders; the trike had indeed performed like new so far.

We walked into the pilots' lounge and there was no one around but we found the urinals and off-loaded coffee to great relief. There was no help posted for how to proceed south and get past the Barry M. Goldwater Gunnery Range restricted air space. Happily, I had prepared somewhat for this possibility, and I had the number of the airport management at the Gila Bend Air Force Auxiliary Airfield (GBN) that was ten miles south of us. Where we sat at the Glia bend Muni we were just on the edge of their sky turf. I would give them a call—I could see no other way to proceed. I knew there was a VRF corridor between Gila bend and Ajo—the next town south—that was in place for civilian flights like ours, but it was not shown on the chart. The chart just shows restricted areas R-2301E butting up against R-2305 with no room in between.

Even I know you may not fly a trike through restricted airspace.

But the chart showed a bit more fine-print information that had been keeping me awake ever since Alfredo showed up with the check and we started planning this trip:

> Permission for flight through R-2305 must be secured from Gila Bend Air Force Auxiliary Field on 127.75 or 122.775. Pilot must have current route map and Gila Bend altimeter setting.

This was enough to keep me awake nights with worry. 1) would Gila Bend Air Force Auxiliary Field grant me the permission I would need to fly through their airspace? There certainly was no other way through—without flying way hell-and-gone for hundreds of miles around the various restricted areas; a possibility I had explored and decided was not a possibility. 2) which frequency would I use to contact GBAFAF, 127.75 or 122.775? This was a question that seemed evident because the chart showed Gila Bend's communications frequency is 127.75. So I wasn't too worried about that. 3) was Gila bend going to require a tail-number before they would give us permission? Because we had no tail-number—we were just an ultralight. 4) would Gila Bend ask for our destination, and—what would I tell them?

Mexico?

One thing I was pretty sure of—if I could just get to the little town of Ajo I would be done with restricted airspace.

I had gleaned the phone number for the air force facility from the airport facilities directory for the southwest and so I dialed the number now. Happily, there was still a pay phone at the airfield.

"Hello," came a voice; "Gila Bend Air Force."

"Hi," I said. "I need permission to fly from the Gila bend municipal to the airfield in Ajo, Arizona. Can you help me?"

"What is your current location?"

"I'm standing in the terminal at the Gila Bend Muni," I said.

"Get in the air and call Snake Eye."

"Get in the air and call Snake Eye?"

"Roger that."

It wasn't exactly the advice I had been hoping for. What I was hoping for is someone who would say something like, *We'll stop the bombers and the straffers, now get going!* Or maybe just, *We'll tell our jet-jockeys not to shoot down any trikes,* but of course they didn't know we were in a trike.

"How do I reach Snake Eye?" I asked, feeling very silly.

"One twenty-seven point seven five," came the answer. It was the frequency from the chart.

"Well," I said. "You see, I'm flying an open-cockpit airplane and I don't communicate so well when I..."

"What's yer tail number?" he asked.

"I don't have a tail number?"

"No tail number? What are you flying?"

"I am flying an ultralight."

"Please hold."

"Espero," I said to Alfredo. *I'm waiting.* I figured he was ready to go even if I wasn't. From Ajo... if we could just get to Ajo... you can smell Mexico from there. Tacos... Burritos... The smell of tacos and burritos was just over the horizon. Mariscos too. Alfredo's advice, if I asked it, was probably to get in the Tanarg, point her nose south and step on the gas. We could use our noses to get where we were going. That's why I didn't ask I guess. I was just on hold with my future in limbo. Suddenly;

"Get in the air and call Snake Eye on one two seven point seven five," said the Voice. "They will give you further instructions."

"Umm… Okay," I said. "Roger that. Call Snake Eye for instructions." I hung up and turned to my amigo. "¡Vamanos!" I said, more optimistically than I felt. I had set the wheels in motion though, I had made the bird fly… There was no backing-down now.

This time Alfredo took the back seat and I sat up front. I would be the pilot now and that would be a little better—although Alfredo is a very competent flier I needed my destiny in my own hands. We warmed up the trike, taxied out to runway two-three, and stepped on the gas. The Tanarg leaped into the sky. Next stop—MEXICO!

~ 𝄞 ≥ ≤ 𝄞 ~

We cruised west around Class D Gila Bend—the air force guys—and then swung south to follow highway eighty-five, headed for R-2305 just a few miles south and the gunnery range just beyond there. When we had settled I gave Alfredo the controls and he began to pilot from the back seat as I tried to contact Snake Eye. Hell, I didn't even know what Snake Eye was, but I didn't like the sound of it. I knew for sure I didn't want to tangle with them, or incur their wrath in any way. I stopped short of praying but held that open as an option.

"Snake Eye. This is ultralight U-F-C two-niner calling Snake Eye. Come in Snake Eye." I felt somewhere between desperate and silly as I broadcast. "Snake Eye, do you read?"

"Roger that ultralight. You got Snake Eye here. What can I do for you today?"

"I am in a civilian aircraft—an ultralight—and I need permission to fly south through R-2305 to Ajo. Can you give me clearance?"

"Umm, please repeat that message ultralight."

"Request clearance to fly south in R-2305 to Ajo, Arizona."

"What is your current location?"

"I'm just south of Gila Bend, flying around Class-D at GBN and approaching Highway 85. I want to turn south."

"Please hold right there," came the answer and, even before I could absorb that reply, he clicked back on again... "How fast does that thing fly?"

"Umm, sixty," I answered.

"Is that knots?" he asked. "Sixty knots?"

"Roger that," I said, even though I didn't know a knot from a hole in my head—I wasn't about to start saying "No" to Snake Eye.

"Hold right there," he said again.

Hold right there...?

How could I *hold right there*?

Happily, there was a nice ridge right in front of us and we were flying through a small pass and I just pointed at some radio towers there and Alfredo, my co-pilot, swung the bar for a turn and soon we were soaring the hill in light ridge-lift. We were able to cut back on throttle a bit and enjoy this early morning soaring. Well, Alfredo enjoyed it. I could see him back there with a shit-eating grin on his face.

"¿Que dicen?" he inquired. *What did they say?*

"Pidieron que esperamos aqui mismo," I explained. *They ordered us to wait right here.*

My co-piloto laughed at this nonsense, but he was the only one of us who felt so light-hearted about our circumstances. How the hell do you hold in an airplane anyway? Put on the brakes, pull off on the shoulder?

Circling, was all I could imagine. Or... soar the tiny ridge, which is what we did. We make figure-eights, swinging back-and-forth along the ridge and trying to milk the light lift.

"¿Por quanto tiempo?" asked Alfie. It was the ten-thousand peso question: *For how long?*

"Fuck I don't know!" I said, and didn't bother to translate, but Alfie gave me a bit of a pat on the back, a show of support.

"Muy bonito mañana agozar," he declared. *Very pretty morning to enjoy.*

I wasn't enjoying it though; I just wanted to get the hell going. What was wrong with these guys?

Just as I was about to grab the mic and see if we had been forgotten the radio buzzed back to life.

"Ultralight, you said you're traveling at sixty knots, correct?"

"About that," I said. Of course, airplanes travel faster or slower depending on winds. "I'll go as fast as I can," I continued, as if that might help.

"Ultralight, follow highway eighty-five heading south and stay at five-hundred feet. Do not deviate."

I could hardly believe it... One moment I was in Limbo, the next I had been liberated. I was Libre!

"Understood Snake Eye and thanks," I said and then, "Wahooo!", this last just through the headsets to my co-pilot. "¡Vamanos!" I said, pointing south.

I grabbed the bar from Alfredo and he dug his video camera out from the seat-pocket. While I followed the instructions from Snake Eye, Alfredo started filming. From here on out we were looking forward to a spectacular adventure, but first we had to get to Ajo.

We held the trike down low and tried to stay over the highway centerline. Now I knew why they wanted the pilot to have the Gila Bend altimeter setting—a detail I had neglected to observe back there on the tarmac. I glanced at the altimeter now and realized that I didn't know how accurate it was, in fact I could surely speculate that it was clearly off to some degree. I knew what five-hundred feet looked like though. We stayed low, and highway eighty-five was like a long emergency runway beneath us with very infrequent traffic. Watching out ahead we saw a flight of four fighter jets swoop down on the desert and drop live bombs on distant targets. We could not hear the explosions, but we could sure as hell see the explosions.

"¡Ve te ala chingada!" said the Mexican.

"Holy shit!" said the gringo.

"No vamos por alla," we agreed with each other.

R-2305 is about thirty miles long and we held the bar to my chest—Alfredo helping out from the back seat—the whole way. We were doing about seventy-miles-an-hour, which I could only hope was fine with Snake Eye. In any event, no jet jokey shot at us, or even approached us, which was good because I might have blown a valve. As we neared the end of the gunnery range we came upon a United States Border Patrol shakedown on the highway below. They were stopping all northbound traffic and looking up their skirts to see what they could find.

Alfredo came on the headsets: "¡Pinche cabrones de la chingada!" he said.

You might say Alfredo was not too fond of these boys. And you would be right too... For years Alfredo had been passing these guys and for years they had been hassling him and for years he had been contemplating some measure of revenge—no matter how slight. Suddenly, he had inspiration provided by opportunity.

"Juu fly bery bery low," he suggested, "Ant eye gib dem ihasta la chingada!" With that, he leaned far out of the back seat to accompany his suggestion with an obscene gesture—what we gringos often call 'the bird'.

I let the nose up then, and we immediately commenced a climb. I did not want to be within even five hundred feet of the US Border Patrol with Alfredo in the back seat of a tiny plane, gesticulating wildly to those below. Maybe they were wondering about us? Maybe they were even now spying on us with binoculars? I did not doubt that—we had seen border patrol vans and trucks all over the place below us—maybe some of them called us in as suspicious characters? But I figured heck, any aircraft traveling south this close to the border was above suspicion—so to speak—of the Border Patrol. In fact, I figured you could do just about anything you wanted with your plane on the border, as long as you kept going south. Drugs? Guns? Bombs? Ultralights? Any thing goes... south.

¡No problema cabrones!

Still, I did not want Alfredo flipping the bird at the feds from five-hundred feet.

"¡Chinga les!" concluded my amigo as we climbed out. Then he laughed heartily.

~~~~~~~~~~~~~~~ _____ ~~~~~~~~~~~~~

Heck, we were nearly through with Snake Eye anyway, beyond his piece of sky in fact. We never heard from him again. We could happily thumb or noses at the stinkin' feds; what might they do, send a chopper for us? An F-16? Fuck 'em! We had completed the hardest part of our flight and we could almost smell the mariscos. It was time for a laugh...

"¡Alli!" said Alfredo, pointing at an imposing volcano on the horizon, about thirty miles south. *There!*

He was pointing at Cerro El Pinacate, beyond which lay our destination. From the back seat, he swung the nose around until it was aimed right for the summit and we forged ahead. If it was up to the gringo we would have driven around the peak following the highway and possibly saving some fuel, but the Mexicano would have nothing of it. Cerro El Pinacate rises from sea-level on the cost, to twelve-hundred meters at its peak and we were flying straight for it.

But first we had to cross the border.

Now, the few times I have crossed this border in a trike I did so at Nogales, where there is just no doubt about where you be. At Nogales, Mexico backs right up to the States with a high-density population and a very distinct fenceline. You look down on that mess of humanity, and you have no doubt which country you're in. But, gazing out in front of us now, our situation was quite unclear. I could see a village up ahead, but where was Lukeville—the Arizona side—and where was Sonoyta, Sonora? Where was the line? There were plenty of lines in the desert but none that really said *border* to me. I guessed it didn't really matter, the die had been cast, we were headed for the sea, and when we crossed an arbitrary line through the desert was not relevant.

¿Verdad?

Well, anyway... We were going in the right direction—south. If we decided to turn back now and head norte, we would probably be intercepted by billions of dollars of high-tech flight-intercept hardware, and we may even be shot down. Flying into Mexico, well... With any luck they might offer us a chilly Tecate when we arrived.

South, then, it was...

I let Alfredo drive while I twisted around in the driver's seat to check our fuel level. The fuel gauge on a Tanarg is a sight-tube and this was the first time I had ever tried to observe the fuel level bouncing around inside that tube, in a critical situation, while actually in flight. I found it very sketchy. In fact, this was the first time I realized that the Tanarg sight-tube fuel gauge is just about worthless. Even while concentrating as well as I might while someone else flew the wing, I could not be sure of our fuel level.

We were in the sixty-thousand dollar trike that has no readable fuel gauge.

"Fuck!" said I, as I turned back to the helm.

"Fuck?" asked Alfie. "¿Como que fuck amigo? Fuck what?"

"Fuck the goddamn fuel level," I said. "Fuckin' bullshit!"

"¿Que pasa?"

"I can't see the gas!" I declared. "I can't see shit!"

Alfredo pointed at the hour meter on the dash, the gauge that had showed one-point-one hours when we began this journey. "Ya tenemos quatro horas de vuelo," he said. *We've been flying for four hours.*

I mulled that over; the Tanarg, with almost seventeen gallons of fuel aboard, should fly for at least six hours even if we ran her hard. We were climbing up on the top of our flight path, the highest point of our flight—Cerro El Pinacate—and we would be there in about a half hour. It would be all downhill from there. We should have plenty of go juice.

"¡Vamanos!" yelled Alfredo, in what had become our mantra. I gazed about and tried to spot somewhere we might put down in case of emergency, but there was none within our glide. At least—there was nowhere I'd like to land. In fact, in retrospect I know that you can't do anything in an airplane near Cerro El Pinacate, except die a horrible death if you are so unlucky as to have to glide to a landing there. For as far as a glider might glide there is nothing but volcanic wasteland, razor-sharp obsidian and volcanic rocks that would tear you apart. Then of course, you would be lost to all but the buzzards. It was a scenario I didn't want to examine too closely.

Happily, I didn't have to. For out in the distance was the big sweeping blue of the Sea of Cortez, inviting us to the popular seaside resort of Puerto Peñasco—our destination. I was amazed how much it had grown since my last visit some years earlier. We were still aiming for the summit of the volcano however, and so I held tight on the bar while we blazed on in. We crested the heights by a hundred feet or so and then pulled the nose down and dove on it—coming within just a foot or two of the crest—until the cone dropped off below us again.

"¡WahOOO!" screamed my amigo.

He cranked a turn then and we made a mild wing-over and swooped back in with that 912 blazing at full-cry. Alfredo had gone a bit loco it seemed, but his exuberance was contagious. We made three or four high-banked wing-overs and then settled into a glide for the beach. You could smell it now on the air. In fact, I thought I could see the distant runway too, although I didn't know for sure.

"¿Tengamos que llamar?" I asked. *Do we have to call in?*

"Sí," said Alfie. "Ciento-vente-siete punto cinco." *Channel one-twenty-seven point five.*

I dialed up the channel and grabbed the mic. But then I realized that we had no real name, no tail-number, nothing that the authorities might recognize. But this is why I had Alfredo along—it was his idea, it was his responsibility, and it was his job to call the airport Comandante. I would have to make the actual call though because it was my headset that had the microphone.

"¿Que dijo?" I asked. *What do I say?*

"Di le que somos Pelicano Uno y que aqui venimos." *Tell him we are Pelican One and here we come.*

"¿Que?" I said, confused. *What?* "¿Pelicano Uno?" I had never heard an aviation call-sign that sounded more like a trucker's.

"Sí, sí," said Alfie. "Somos Pelicano Uno y aqui llegamos. ¡Di le!" *Yes, yes. We are Pelican One and here we're on arrival. Tell him!*

I felt silly as I keyed the mic and said, "Puerto Peñasco, Puerto Peñacso somos Pelicano Uno y somos a diez millas al norte y llegamos para aterrizar." *Rocky Point, Rocky Point this is Pelican One and we are ten miles north and inbound to land.*

Imagine my relief then, as our call was quickly returned.

"Bienvenido Pelicano Uno, toma pista dos-nueve, vientos calmado." *Welcome Pelican One, take runway two-nine, winds are calm.*

With Alfredo pointing the way we entered the pattern and looked down on the apron where a small crowd had gathered.

"Aquellos son," said my co-pilot. *That's them.*

"¿Quien?" I asked.

"Es el dueño y sus amigos. Esperen su avioncito Nuevo." *The owner and his friends. They await his new trike.*

We flew a quick base and chopped throttle for a steep approach to a round-out. Alfredo sat in the back seat and waved a greeting to the crowd below. We skimmed the runway in nice smooth air and greased a landing. We stopped on the runway and turned a one-eighty to head back towards the small crowd.

"¿Qual es el dueño?" I asked. *Which one is the owner?*

"Es él," said Alfie pointing. "Señor Gregorio, con el cuero." *Mr. Gregory, in the leather.*

Indeed, in the middle of the crowd stood a tall man, distinguished-looking, and wearing a black leather jacket. This was the man who had spent sixty-grand and more on this trike and who was now in charge of our welcoming committee. I felt like I had to impart a little drama to the scene...

So I stepped on the gas and goosed that Tanarg with the nose down so she would not take off. Then I shut down the spark—to stop the prop—and pulled the keys from the dash. With the keys in hand now, and the crowd about to dive out of the way, I banked the wing and pushed the fork for a hard left turn and made a neat three-sixty show-off circle that brought me back to the crowd, now nice and slow. I tossed the keys at the leather jacket himself—hitting him right in the chest. Señor Gregorio snatched the keys as they fell and stood grinning happily back at us.

Pelicano Uno had landed.

Epilogue, Taking Mexico Flying

As it turned out MEXICO was far too large for his harness. He took MEXICO flying once and it made a horrible tender spot over his heart, right where his glove box was. He was laying on MEXICO and he kept having to pushup on the bar to relieve the pressure and in fact, he feared the *guantero* zipper might just pop right open and he'd lose MEXICO forever, somewhere over Mexico. He put down in a field of jamaica flowers and realized some better arrangement would have to be made.

That's when it came to him—he would tear MEXICO apart. It was just a cheap paperback after all; dog-eared and tattered. He thought he'd paid a quarter for it back in Tucson, or maybe four bits. He opened it to page one thousand twelve—exactly half of MEXICO, and he cut it in two with his machete.

That seemed appropriate.

Much more comfortable too.

But one thousand pages was still pretty big. He noticed that the first hundred pages or so were just barely hanging in there; the spine was frazzled along the edge and the pages were about to fall off. He turned to page seventy-three—just as much as he'd read thus far—and tore them off too. <u>MEXICO</u> was getting better all the time. That was when the notion came to him...

He would scatter Mexico with <u>MEXICO</u>! He would tear off every page as he read it and just toss it to the wind. <u>MEXICO</u> would get smaller every day.

Plus, litter was no big thing in Mexico, he would be just another litterbug, only on a very small scale. It would be like getting some measure of revenge on Mexico, with <u>MEXICO</u>.

Better yet, his litter would have cultural value too, which is about the best you could say about Michener's <u>MEXICO</u>—a very boring read indeed. His litter would not be just the typical Mexican litter you see laying about and gathering in piles everywhere—plastic bottles and plates and bags and glass and all sorts of consumer packaging, furniture and appliances and cars and spent durable goods. Not to mention the far-worse stuff... Garbage, along with all the trash.

<u>MEXICO,</u> the written word, would be scattered across the land...

Quickly, he read through a page and tossed it to the viento. It blew across the road and stacked up with some other trash, trash that was of absolutely no interest whatsoever, thrash that was unlikely to degrade organically for hundreds of years—maybe thousands...

Shit howdy, why hadn't he thought of this long before?

~~~~~~

Hasta la vista amigos!
www.TalesFromTheWildBlueYonder.com

Ole@LearnToHangGlide.com

~~~~~~~~~~~~~~~~ ~~~~~~~~~~~~~~~~

www.ingramcontent.com/pod-product-compliance
Lightning Source LLC
Chambersburg PA
CBHW070050260626
47160CB00004B/1165